dear
dead person

short fiction by

benjamin weissman

SERPENT'S TAIL

HIGH
RISK
BOOKS

NEW YORK / LONDON

This collection first published by
High Risk Books/Serpent's Tail
4 Blackstock Mews, London, England N4 2BT
and 401 West Broadway, New York, N.Y. 10012

Library of Congress Cataloging-in-Publication Data

Weissman, Benjamin, 1957–
        Dear dead person : short fiction / by Benjamin Weissman.
                  p.   cm.
        ISBN 1-85242-330-7
        1. Title
        PS3573.E4168D4   1994   94-2086
        813 ' .54—dc20   CIP

Book and cover design by Rex Ray
Typeset in Janson 11/15 and Futura Condensed by *Loos Amalgam*
Printed in Hong Kong by Colorcraft, Ltd.

                10 9 8 7 6 5 4 3 2

Frontispiece:
Benjamin Weissman,
Eat, 1993, ink on paper, 8½ x 11
Collection of Roy Dowell and Lari Pittman

for Amy Gerstler

Roll call. Extreme, worshipful, cannot-live-without thanks to Vater, Mutter, und Schwester (Murray, Gracia, Julie), and to godhead colleagues and super pals Lisa Anne Auerbach, Charles Baxter, Bernard Cooper, Roy Dowell, Dana Duff, David Humphrey, Tom Knechtel, Kate Knuth, Peter Kogler, Jim Krusoe, Timothy Martin, Renee Petropolous, Lari Pittman, Trace Rosel, Amy Scholder and Ira Silverberg, Alexis Smith, Thaddeous Strode, Lynne Tillman, and Christopher Williams—your brains and heart are wildly appreciated, especially Amy Gerstler, Dennis Cooper, and Lane Relyea, who went over every page of this thing.

Contents

Contents

It doesn't take much to show love, but at some time or another in your, praise God, disastrous life, you must have felt, honestly and simply, what love is and how love likes to behave.

—Robert Walser

dear
dead person

Pushed

YOU RETURN HOME from a horrible day at work. You refuse to say what it is you do. You say, I don't do anything. It's too painful, too bland and pitiful. You say, I should quit. They're going to fire me, I know it. As you walk down the street people step in front of you and then stop. You're supposed to get the idea, without anyone uttering a sound, to walk around the person—but then this happens a second time, a third, fourth, fifth; people stepping out into the world for a serious bit of informal wandering, their destination unspecified. No doubt these people are headed somewhere, but the odd pacing of their steps indicates an irregularity. They blunder in front of you and stop. They check their watches, feel around in their pockets. You say, Have I forgotten anything? Yes, they say they have, but they can't remember what. You say, It's not that important. I'll live without it. *(Buy dog food.)* They look up at the sky. Mustn't forget to acknowledge nature. Five thousand years ago that's all there was: sky, trees, mud, and more sky. Nature exclusive. Large, dangerous animals everywhere, and naked people fighting with branches and rocks. Everybody worried. During all this you are standing there like an immobile iceberg who's slammed on the brakes. We are not all the same. There are differences so great that some of us must be of the reptile family. You think of hissing or beeping, or saying something, like Move, or Out of my way, Bub. Bub is a beautiful word, and it has disappeared from our vocabulary. No one uses it anymore. You think of striking this person, of ramming or denting them. As you try and pass someone on the left, he suddenly leans in that direction. You try the right side and up swings an elbow. One moment it's a man (all coughs, dandruff and briefcase) whose chiseled leathery face looks like a lizard; the next, another man, who looks like a woman; the next, an older heavy-set woman who bares a horrifying resemblance to Rod Steiger. You come across a trio of four-foot old ladies (massive and gloomy). These constant observers of illness and death radiate an ominous quality. And then there are children who clutter the sidewalks, and, in their anarchy, destroy life. They loosen every screw the adults have tightened. Bless all their hearts, but not if they step in front of you and stifle progress. No. The clocks continue to tick. You can feel it now. You are stretched as if you were a thick piece of rubber. People are forward-moving creatures; to stop them in any way is to ruin them. They rust, rot and curdle within a short period of time. One would think one could, or should, push these road blocks out of the way. Isn't that one of our rights as people? But you don't, because it's impolite, inappropriate, out of the question. Retaliation could result in a swifter, more brutal punishment, a slower, more fiendish death. As foul and untruthful as politeness often is, in most cases it is also a necessity that must be strictly enforced. The grizzily world doesn't need another indiscreet monster added to the roster, knocking people down to get from point A to point B. And so you pause and take in a long breath. The air inside your chest tastes like honeydew melon. Is that possible? It's green and sweet. Your throat is wet. Your chest fills with air. You exhale. You are strong. You are alive. All this helps, it's a diversion, but after the twenty-third slowdown incident you are beyond repair. People. You say the word, you spit it out. How much angrier can you get? People, they are like worms. You think, I have a temper. I'm boiling over. You think, I thought I lengthened my fuse when I graduated from high school. All your anger did was get you into trouble: a grunter, a teeth-gritter, a reputation for turning red. You frightened people and now you are a calm, repressed soul—or were before this problem started. Then there was a period when you wanted it back, the rage, because you thought it gave you strength. People ran away. They returned in larger numbers. A mad version of yourself, like the drunken fool, could conquer anything. It did, but all you accomplished were travesties. You dug holes. You made a big mess. You wasted time cleaning up. You lost friends, burned bridges. You let your enemies know what you really thought of them. All they did was take note and smile. But no one ever took a swing at you. Even so, you got swollen and puffy and discolored, all on your own, just from sitting around. A stagnant citizen. Now, when you walk into a room people look at you like you have excrement smeared on your face. And you do. I am a shit face, you say, a shit head, a shit hole, a shit brain. You are weary from this line of thinking. But these kinds of thoughts escort you to your apartment. You climb the steps, force yourself to think of nothing. The hallway smells like it always has, like a stew of congealed, oily meats, with pockets of vibrant, obscene urine. The smell goes straight into your brain like a lethal vapor. Your thighs serve you well, even if they are shapeless and unmuscular. Soon it will be summer and everyone will wear shorts. You say, compared to me, even obese people, three hundred pound lardy cows, look good in shorts. I'm starchy. They're sturdy and grand, their bellies tight like the skin stretched over an enormous drum. You say, I'm stale, small, gooey, bruised, and brittle, and at home you have one thing to look forward to: the eating of a favorite cookie. For some reason this pleasure has grown, like the aforementioned agonies, out of proportion. You know what this cookie tastes like. You've eaten them a thousand times. They are large triangles of flour, the size of your hand; inside is a lightly sweetened cherry filling. One could say it is like a little personal pie. Everything about this cookie brings you happiness: the tranquil, reassuring smell of the dough, the intensity of the cherries. You eat it in bed, with a glass of milk. As despicable as any day might be, there is always this cookie to stand there, in the end, and defend you, to fall into your stomach and say, I'm yours, I love you. To some extent that's what this is all about. An absence of tenderness. This lonesome, furious individual, who storms through life (this is still you, the trial is endless), holds his own edible form of God in his hands. It is the glorious cookie, cerebral and sanctified. It is noble. It is perfection. But when you step into your apartment, something is wrong. The dog, who's been inside all day, the other you, the small furry man, the one you have to take out for a walk, who needs dinner *(forgot to buy dog food)*, is standing on your bed. Yes, something is very wrong. Everything slows down. The bag from the bakery, beside your dog. He's guarding it like a prize. But the bag is torn open, crumbs are everywhere, with little spots of cherry filling on your pillow. This is what life has come down to. It wants to drill you into the ground and seal you up for good. First the world steps in front of you and slows you down to a crawl, and then your dog destroys the cookie. He ate it out of curiosity, from a bag that he knew held special importance. The cookie was just there. There was nothing better to do. You start in on the dog. You say, loudly... actually, you are screaming...at your dog...at 8 P.M., Who do you think you are? What the fuck is your problem? You stupid little motherfucker. That cookie was for me. Dogs don't eat cookies. They're bad for you. Cookies will kill you. I will kill you. I need that cookie. I live for that fucking thing. Now you are alarming the neighbors, and that's just fine, because this is hopeless and tragic. The neighbors never heard you make a sound before. You are single. You live alone, with the dog. To the neighbors you are a sad and friendly man. Your face is lined with grief. You stop. It's too painful. You want to cry but you can't. Your dog is looking the other way. He's ashamed, he cowers, he admits to the crime, he knows he ate the love of your life, it's true, and now he would like to be your friend again, or within the next five minutes. You sit down beside him and speak gently into his face. Asshole, you whisper, asshole, asshole. The dog licks you. The world is always saying, forgive your dog, he means you no harm. But that's not true, because he just broke the biggest rule of all. He swallowed your cookie. You say, I am wounded, weakened, defeated. Tonight, nothing can replace this cookie. An ice cream or a Bon Bon is a sick joke right now. You stare at the cherry-stained pillow. You rub your head. Someone help me. You flip the pillow over. The other set of sheets are in the dirty clothes pile. You turn off the light and get into bed with all your clothes on. No one eats. As a child you'd often do this, sleep fully dressed, pop up in the morning like the fireman you wanted to be, strong and cheerful. But there are crumbs everywhere. They feel like gravel. Your bed is a little sandbox. The dog steps around your body and curls into a spot on the bed farthest from you. Everyone's going to rest. Your heart is beating throughout your body. You can feel it in your arms, inside your eyes and lips. Your face is like a bleeding organ and it needs to be covered or else it will leak. The comforting linen pillow is now only a cruel reminder of what has happened. The only way you could fall asleep is if you slammed a frying pan over your head, and once asleep your dreams would return to the cookie. The women from the bakery would all be your neighbors. You run into a cave where there's a bakery. You smell the dough. For a second you see the cookie and then lose it. Now it's on the wall as decoration. People, of course, step in front of you. The line is moving but your feet are stuck. People are walking the other way with crumbs falling out of their mouths. You heave rocks to defend

9

yourself, but no matter how hard you throw, the rocks only roll off your fingers and land at your feet. Your bleeding toes attract a lineup of the earth's most unsavory animals, starting with scorpions, rats and wild boars. The boars, slobbering and maniacal, charge at you from a great distance and slam into your stomach. Finally you are in the middle of nowhere, as always, and a group of nasty, impatient vultures awaits your death. But you don't dream anything because you're not going to fall asleep. The only one resting peaceful is the dog. He's already snoring. You are awake. You are forced to look at time, in the darkness of your bedroom, as if it were an eight-hour documentary. In this grainy version each frame moves four times slower than normal, and when you stand up in the morning you will be exhausted.

Confident Mother

EVER SINCE I WAS a tiny girl I knew what I wanted to be and it never changed. My best friends wanted to be cocktail waitresses, French horn players, horse riders, ballerinas. I wanted to be a mother. Nothing else. Only a mother. But I knew when I was little that it wasn't a side thing. All my friends said, Yeah, yeah, I want to be a mother, too. Everyone's a mother. Not so. Completely wrong. Though I suppose throughout history exceptions could be found. I could find anything. This idea made me an adult very quickly. All I needed was a good boy to link up with, but there was none. In the meantime I mothered smooth stones, dead mice and birds. I would rub their bellies and lay them on beds of leaves. I kissed them and told them stories, said everything would be alright. A mother must be positive. Curlers in my hair, darning a holey sock, all my babies were happy. Being the patient girl that I am, I waited and quietly hunted until I found the right man, and he was fine. We married. He loved the idea of starting a family, until I got pregnant. My big belly frightened him off. What kind of love was that? Bad love, so good riddance. I'm sure it was jealousy, the need for undivided attention. Jealousy is a key ingredient in all romances. It heats things up, but then things spoil. Columbus, who is said to have officially discovered America, was jealous of Leif Eriksson. Who cares what the books say? I still believe it was Leif's discovery. Searching. No one stops. I don't stop. I was talking to my boy in my belly—singing to him about everything that was going on around us, explaining the jokes. Laying off alcohol and pot cleared my complexion. And I could see better. Now I could really focus. I drew pictures of kangaroos. Although I didn't hop, I felt like one. We'd go to the park, I'd eat a peanut butter and lettuce sandwich on whole wheat and watch people and be watched. I felt like a public sculpture. The community touched my belly—they pressed their ears to it; they said, You're right, there's a boy in there. Sure enough, when the time came, my man, the boy, popped out. Yes, a lot of pain. I wanted it. I was ready. My boy my boy my boy... all mine. I fed him and changed his diapers. All day long, past the point of agony, he drank milk out of my chest. He was a quiet boy, not a screamer. I took him for walks to the liquor store. He'd pick up broken beer bottles and never cut himself. He had good sense. He'd look right into my eyes and scowl. He knew what was up. He played with all the toys I got him and he had an appetite for whatever little foods I was serving. And he grew fast. In no time I had to get rid of the stroller and the crib and it seemed like every week we had to go to the Goodwill to buy larger clothes. I helped him with his homework, even when he told me it wasn't necessary. He was on the track team in high school. He ran the mile and usually won. I went to every meet. I screamed *go* from the first row of bleachers all over the county. Thinking that food fortifies, I'd eat a hot dog with onions, popcorn, a milk, and a bag of M&M's. In some way I was responsible for his victories. Every Friday and Saturday night we went to the movies. If one of his pals wanted to joint us, that was fine. I would treat. He knew good boys. One day he asked if a girl could join us. The question struck me as so odd. I tried to restrain myself but I was breaking out all over. Hidden nerves raced through my face. My shoulders locked up, I got itchy, my asshole closed shut like an ill sunflower. I said, Let's just the two of us go out tonight, what do you say? My son didn't protest. But the same question arose again the following night: could this *she* join us? I asked him who this girl was and he said, Just a girl. Uh huh, just a girl. Alright, bring her along. He's not a baby anymore. He's a very large young man. He shaves every morning. He belches like a bear. The girl was very polite but I knew what she was thinking, and she knew I knew. That's why her hands remained tightly clasped, and when my son reached for her she giggled and said, Later. Yes, that's right, much later, when the old lady's not around. But that little bitch is in for a surprise. I'm not going anywhere. The problem was my son couldn't stop thinking about her. He visited her twice a day. The thought of her sent him flying down the street, and if I tried to detain him by setting up a program of chores, he'd finish them doubletime. I'd reward him with a tall glass of milk and a pile of cookies, but no, he wasn't hungry. Sure he was hungry, he was hungry for her. That girl lifts up her skirt and stuffs him with more than he can eat. That's the drug: assorted meats and cheeses. Nightmares grow fast and thick—a fire with no air to breathe—just smoke and confusion—time speeded up for multiple conclusions. My head hurt. All I could think about was my son's penis inside that spidery, evil girl, her nails running down his back, her slimy tentacles sucking out all the goodness I put in. I washed that penis. I taught him how to aim his urine. The day after high school graduation I found a note: DEAR MOM, PAM AND I HAVE GONE TO MEXICO TO GET MARRIED. SEE YOU SOON. DON'T WORRY. LOVE, YOUR SON. I wanted to shoot her. To kill her. I wanted to kill that girl. Look what she made him do now. He was gone.

She'd stolen my baby. At the liquor store, I picked up a fifth of whiskey. The same irritating hoodlums were hanging around outside. Then suddenly, glory be, a brainstorm. How would those two boys like to make a little extra money—say, one hundred dollars apiece? Sure they would. I took them back to the apartment and fixed them a nice hot lunch and discussed logistics and the method. Finally I said: I want that bitch's head cut off. I need it off. Her head persuaded my son to leave home. Shoot her first, I don't care. Just make sure the head hits the dirt. Leave the eyes open, don't make no difference. This calmed me a bit, knowing that there would be a change. As soon as the newlyweds returned I dashed to the liquor store and gave my little helpers the green light. Pam and my son came over for dinner that night. I couldn't take my eyes off her. I got such a thrill knowing this was her last day on earth. Her mouth was saying something sweet about my salad dressing. Sure, she could have the recipe. Copy down the one for green tomato pie and chocolate sauerkraut cake, as well. Now's the time to learn everything. After dessert I asked my son to screw in a few out-of-reach lightbulbs. He does that so well. Then they said good night and drove off to Pam's apartment, a twenty-minute drive. I bit my nails. I stared at the clock: the second hand moved like a cripple. I could see them in the car. The girl working on all my boy's parts. I'm certain she was orally copulating him, and he, desperately steering to

15

keep the car on the road, trying to avoid a head-on collision. I see how it works. I'm not afraid to speak up. I know when I'm needed. And being resourceful in an emergency is a human necessity. It's intuitive, chemical, the muse tells me. Once I was certain they were back at her apartment I phoned my son and in a frantic voice begged him to return immediately, to fix my leaky stove. I smelled gas. I was being asphyxiated. He assured me he'd return here in a flash. I hung up the phone and pictured him throwing on his coat and running out the door. He drove off, not knowing he was being watched by my two industrious friends. They knocked on the front door and one of them said, I forgot my keys, honey. Let me in quick. And it worked. She opened the door and they pounced on her. They beat her like a rug and cut her like an animal. A complete ending. A stop to it all. End of romance. My son, all to myself, just like in the beginning. Kiss your mother. Return to my breast. I heard my son's car drive up. Uh-oh, almost forgot about my leaky stove. I ran to the kitchen and blew out the broiler pilot light. I turned it on full-tilt and ran out of the apartment waving my arms, coughing. My sweet son dashed up the stairs, asked if I was alright and then zoomed into the kitchen. He smelled the gas, too. He fixed it. He said it was only a pilot light. Thank God. How could I be so silly? Good to have a man around the house. He rolled his eyes, gave me a big kiss and left. He returned to Pam but she was dead and bloody and in two unequal parts. That's no wife. The police talked to us with clipboards for a couple hours. Slept better than I have in years. Wonderful dreams of my son—the two of us together in ponds, flying, eating... In the morning a detective in jeans asked me to come with him down to the station. More questions. He handcuffed me. Ouch, very painful for the thick-wristed. He had already apprehended the two dumbbells. A jury convicted the two boys and myself of murder—all to get the gas chamber. For two years I sat in a prison cell, surrounded by innocent criminals, like myself, regular ladies. My son visited me every day. He didn't hate me. Our bond could never be broken. But then my son informed me about another girl he'd been seeing. He said they planned to get married. He begged me not to get angry. How could I not? What was he trying to do to me? That's what I wanted to know.

A German Moment

THERE ARE MANY occurrences we never forget, but there is always one big one that links up with history and its flabbergasting menu of horrors. Allow me to proceed. I crawled into the back seat of a small car. A Honda. (We bombed them. How do we atone for that?) I was with two other people: one of them drove and the other was a passenger, like me, except I was in the back alone and felt like the luggage—but when I imagined a large suitcase on the seat by itself it sat less precariously than my bent-up carcass. Human cargo is troublesome. At certain moments being tucked into an embryonic ball can be comforting, but that's probably my screwed up desire to be a kitty. The driver, a man with a mustache as thick as a broom—one I doubt I could ever grow even if I were given an uninterrupted grooming year and treated with special follicle ointments—a thought based simply on the evidence of the hair that sprouts from my forearms, thighs and shins (barely any)—this man, who has more hair on the two square inches above his lip than I have on my entire body, pointed out two old ladies walking gingerly down the street and said, Let me tell you about the German moment I shared with those two frauleins. They are German and they are very sweet. A mother and daughter. I was walking Spencer, my huge dog. So I'm walking along and the older woman looks at me very seriously and asks in her very thick accent, Vat *race* is he, the doggie? For a minute I didn't know what she was saying, but then I figured she meant what *breed*, so I said, Oh, a Labrador. The women nodded and walked on. The driver/storyteller turned the car around and we passed the two women again. The younger one looked at us blankly. My friend waved as the older woman said something while staring at her feet. Nazis pride themselves on knowing how to detect a Jew. We talk, act and look a certain way, all of us. My grandparents were born in Austria. On Saturday mornings I listen to a radio show broadcast from Orange County. German folk music. The authentic host speaks softly, only in German. He pronounces each word slowly, for those learning the language I suppose, not like Hitler, who shrieked rapidly, for those well-versed and hungry for social change. A groggy accordion starts up, and then some singing with lots of *ein* and *und*. Song after song, they all sound the same, but I don't listen carefully. It's difficult to get off the Holocaust channel because it's on the consciousness network twenty-four hours every day, forever. Landscape painting, beer steins and those well-made cars. The Holocaust channel will always be popular because it's still so new, happened only yesterday and nothing is simpler or more confusing than exterminating people.

Museum Boy

TODAY I ENJOY MY father's scrambled eggs just as much as any other day. First he cracks the eggs into a bowl and pitches the runny shells at the sink. He never misses, but the egg whites streak the counter. I wipe that up. We're a team. Then, with a fork and never with a whisk, he beats the eggs until they're full of bubbles. He cooks the eggs loose, adding cheddar from the beginning so the cheese is integrated with the eggs, instead of resting on top like a gooey sheet. It feels good to know the correct word for something. I remember when I first learned to read I felt like a secret agent with wild chemicals.

My mother times her exercises, shower and walk around the block so that she can be in the kitchen alone just as we've finished (in her eyes) breaking things and groveling like animals. I think my father and I are gentlemen. We don't lick our plates. I don't. I haven't licked my plate in a long time. But we do sneeze from the pepper and burp a lot. I love the sound of my father's burps. They tell me the world is well. Once we've finished eating, my mom can sit down to a pure and peaceful hard-boiled egg and burnt toast and marmalade. I hate marmalade but I have a feeling I might appreciate it when I'm older. But how will I get older? Same goes for coffee and whiskey. My smiling parents drink it and say *ahhh* and I wonder if they're fooling me. I smell it; I know it's worse than piss or poop, which actually smell good to me. Maybe not good, but I sure laugh a lot when people talk about it, and they always do. Many things are top-secret; it's just the way things are. I must stay out of trouble. When I'm older will the reverse happen, I wonder? Will I fall out of love with chocolate Coke and chocolate pudding and chocolate graham crackers?

My father scrambles the eggs, nervously stirring them too often. An egg can practically cook itself—for example, on the sidewalks of Texas. I'm in charge of the toast. My father shouts *now toast* and swings an arm, cueing me to lower the toast. We're eating pumpernickle today; black bread, so if I burn it, it won't be so obvious. I spread butter on their faces the second they pop up. I hold the knife in my left hand. I'm a lefty: I open doors, scratch my head and throw tomatoes with my left hand. But no one will shake hands with a lefty. That's because the world thinks we're warlocks. My father shoves the giant wooden spoon in his mouth after he's distributed our portions. I know that big bite will be the best bite of the day. We pepper our eggs and eat. He reads the newspaper. I look out the window. I see cars and birds. Neither of us chokes.

The things my parents have taught me thus far stick to me like a unique disease, never to go away. I speak their language, their weird words fall into my head and land in the middle of my stomach. In that sense most of these words are my own, but not all of them, yet. I guess I follow my parents blindly. I'm grateful I can. If they jumped out of a window or socked an elephant, so would I. A bad imitation of them can be spectacular even though I feel hints of agony at my lack of perfection—it's amazing how often I mess up—not to mention my lack of height. Standing up, my chin lines up with an adult belly-button. That's what's really horrible, my point of view. When I was littler I thought people lost their bellybuttons when they got real old. Another theory shattered.

My father is a master, like any father.

Today is Sunday. Church. I don't hate church. I don't hate the singing (it's funny the way it sounds like crying) but it embarrasses me to sing, because I sing so badly. A teacher at school told me so. I stare at the old people, the ones about to die. They seem like they should all be in bed. Why would anyone be afraid of dying? How much different from sleeping could it be? No nightmares. I hate bedtime, so I could kind of see the dread. I like staring at people's hands and feet. Big brown shoes. Eyes too. They're like marbles with ideas.

After church we're going to the museum. I've never been to a museum before. I don't know why I don't like doing things I've never done before. It worries me. My patience goes—it's irritating, dumb. It's like when a substitute teacher asks me a lot of questions. I don't like to be forced to think on the spot about something I'm not sure I care about, by someone who'll be gone tomorrow and forever.

I HAVE A GIANT DOG named Sonar. He's a collie. I ride him to school along the sidewalk. We go slower than the cars. Sonar is too big to live inside the house so he sleeps under my window. To be honest, Sonar isn't really my dog. But he followed me home once and I fed him. First water, then milk, eggs, bread and leftover pizza. He didn't go until I went to bed. My parents say no animals. This is a restriction I find difficult to live with. They say when I'm older I can live with all the animals I want. In another galaxy, they mean. My parents say I can't have a dog because it'll destroy the curtains and carpet. The dog will decrease the value of the house.

The first week of my life I lived in the top dresser drawer where my father kept his socks. Then my parents bought a crib, and for the next year I lived soiled and clean, soiled and clean, behind bars. I remember lying on my back knowing that one day I'd be too big for that feeble prison, that I'd be moved again, to something larger, something without bars. It's good to be an infant. I didn't mind it at all. Reports were that I was tolerable. But I was fat and had to go on an early diet. Skim milk. That's embarrassing. I was content with the limitations of early life and I loved the flies that landed on me. They made me laugh, not knowing they were menacing things that must be routinely slapped to death with a swatter. I was a wordless blob in a white fluffy nest. Red lips on giant, square faces descended and periodically suffocated me.

I want to go to hell because in hell the dead run around with no clothes and I can spend all day staring. A gloomy butt appears to ask for the simplest things. Wipe me. Bite me. Shall I go? When I watch my parents kiss and fuck I wonder why they don't fart and cry, with their butts in the air, groaning like perturbed goats. My father's always on top. His hairy back covers any trace of mom. They resemble a seething science project: formless and troubling. In hell I'll run around naked and be my very own cartoon character, jumping over lakes of fire, swinging from the veins of Satan, spearing devils.

I'd like to be Tarzan in Africa. I like Jane. I like Tarzan's monkey friends and his elephant. I wouldn't want to be Superman in New York.

I KNOW THERE ARE paintings and sculptures in the museum. I read in the newspaper about the museum buying a modern painting for two millions dollars. The article said even a child could've painted it. I also know that buying a painting for so much money is supposed to shock me like a big murder, but it doesn't. I hardly ever read the newspaper except when I'm assigned to write a current events report for civics class. After reading what the article said about adults painting as bad as a kid, I waited till after lunch to make sure both my parents were done reading the paper so I could punch holes in the writer's name with a pencil and then break the lead over his first initials.

My father says two million dollars is abstract, like clouds. I leave that alone. I'm not uncomfortable being left in the dark. I close my eyes and no one can see me, so we're even, but I begin to see new things that I only see with my eyes shut: a special toy bird with a giant beak that doesn't kill me; the bird glides

motionless with its wings still, a showering of burst-
ing lightbulbs, upside-down cars that drive from roof
to roof.

I see paintings everywhere. Paintings are pictures made with paint. I know that sounds silly but it's
true. We paint at school. I paint better than I sing.
That isn't my opinion, it's the higher mark on my
report card. My mom keeps all my report cards in a
drawer by the telephone in the kitchen. That drawer
is filled with a ton of sharpened pencils. The music
instructor stopped me after five seconds when I tried
out for the school chorus. He said stop right there,
good-bye, the chorus will be better off without you.
This man deserved a beating but he was right. I don't
know why I tried out in the first place. It seemed
weird and a little fun. I could disguise myself and
hide out in the back row, carry on my shady dealings
yet appear to harmonize with the others.

Maybe I'm an angry boy. It's possible.

Even though we all know that the world is
round there are still many things that tell us that this
is untrue, that the world is very flat. People fall off all
the time.

I like to paint. I like the wetness, moving it
around. I always paint the same thing though: a knife
jammed into a face, lots of blood spurting out. I paint
the blood as if it were tears or raindrops. My friends
like it but my teacher doesn't; she thinks I should

work on something different, a landscape. I know I go to school, like other children, under the idea that something will catch onto me, or that I'll grab on to it, and that I'll become great at this one thing and it'll carry me through life. Paying the bills, keeping a big smile. All I need is one subject. I always get B's in handwriting.

There are sculptures all over the city. They pop out of the ground like freaks of nature, or the remains of a happy airplane crash.

Sunday is a day I never get to mess around with my friends. After church we usually go to a weird aunt or uncle's house, or some other geek's, and eat something. Last Sunday I broke a ukulele string and my uncle told my dad that he'd just bought himself a guitar. My mom made a face when he said that. She says he always does things to humiliate my dad. Should I kill him? We hang around after the services, everyone nodding their heads. I don't know anyone and I don't want to. I want to go home and throw a ball up to the sky. For church I dress up like a toy businessman. At home I sit on the stoop with my father, waiting for my mom. He calls her a glorious woman. She resembles the ladies in the magazines she buys. We cheer and slap her five when she leaves the house. We both tell her she looks nice (she has a gallon of perfume on and she smells nice, too). She thanks us and asks why we insist on leaving the door open, inviting in all the flies.

My mom tears a month off the calendar: every month of every year stored in a secret place (in the back of the closet, in a hat box, underneath smelly old blankets). Late at night when we're all asleep (not me) my mom says things to the old months the same way she does to old photographs in the afternoon on the porch. She talks directly to them, shakes her head, kisses them and cries. Pictures of her dead parents, dead cousins, pictures of herself when she was my age. I've seen all the pictures. Everyone looks sad and their clothes are brown and baggy. I don't think my mom's crazy just because she talks to paper. I talk to plenty of people who never say a word back.

I took my bed out for a spin. My bed can be transformed into an aircraft. The control panels are all along my belly. I'm the only trained pilot. I usually hover the block for a while before cruising the city. Just after takeoff I caught my mom out on the porch, crying. I don't know what about, but for some reason it didn't seem deadly, that it was a good cry, if there is such a thing. My mom is a quiet person, like my father; they only say what they must. Most of their talk is done with their eyes—long, complex communications—and then suddenly they speak and it's only Yes, dear, or I wish things were that simple… I'm like that too. I don't talk to anyone for a real long time, but I've covered a lot of ground inside my head and none of it needed to come out.

SUNDAY MOVES BY very slowly, everything takes forever. I could dig my own grave and bury myself in dirt before a neighbor finishes a sentence. We're invited to another house for lunch, but my father said no, today we're going to the museum.

My mother drives, my father navigates. He instructs her to be careful, to change lanes, to turn left and right. There's always a shortcut. This is my father's city. He's seen it in miniature. From office building towers, from airplanes, in his head when he concentrates. He has an overview. Park there, he says. My father knows exactly which parking space is the best. How did he learn all this?

We lock our doors carefully. My father stares at the car as if it suddenly changed colors. The walk through the sculpture garden feels weightless and pure. There's one thing that looks like it should appeal to someone my age. It's a giant steel mobile in red, yellow and black. I don't like it. It's probably called *Gouchy-goo in Babyland*. Without touching me it pinches my cheek like the hairy wart lady at the fruit market. One day I will punch her in the stomach. In my head I already have. There's another sculpture: a pile of logs neatly stacked on top of each other. Toys for a cyclops, I guess. Maybe they're charged with electrical volts and if I touch one I'll die. I like that.

A man is playing the flute. The sounds sneak through the leaves in the trees and seep into the moist earth that keeps the trees from flying away.

30

That's a poem. Thank you. At the musician's feet there's a pie tin with coins and dollar bills. I have a quarter. I think I'll contribute the quarter to his greatness even if his music does sound sort of dumb and sweet, like little fairies skipping around.

A brick pathway weaves through a bumpy slope of grass. My parents make pained faces as they duck their heads to avoid low-hanging branches. I wonder if there are squirrels up there. Squirrels are as dangerous as rats, which scare me more than lions and great white sharks. I know that's dumb. Rats eat the same foods we do and people resent that. People love squirrels, they're the charm of every community. The darling squirrel performs tightrope acts on tele-phone wires; it nibbles neatly on walnuts. They're full of disease. They transmit rabies. I knew a boy who had those rabies shots in the stomach. Each shot—nine in all, one per week—made his stomach swell up and hurt. The boy was actually a grown man; they usually never cry but these shots turned him into a baby and he almost died. I didn't know this man; I read about him in Time magazine at the beauty par-lor. My mom drags me along. I learn things there.

When I was ten I wrote a book called *Operation: Kill*. It was about a ten-year-old detective named Bobby Kill, the toughest fifth grader Wonderland Elementary had ever seen. He uncov-ered the elusive eraser thief and dragged him to the principal's desk. Kill caught the Rock brothers pounding the student body president to death. Kill was small and only ten but he had a slingshot and deadly aim to boot, which forced troublemakers to think twice. He had a scream that paralyzed adults, he could run fast and he didn't hate girls. My second book was called *Troubles a Turtle May Face*. It was about the serious obstacles for a fragile turtle. Flipped over on his back, asked to participate in races, thrown into cauldrons, and so on. These books are only available in my room.

Are you hungry, Max? my mother asks me.

No, I say.

We are. Would you mind if we grab a quick bite at the cafeteria?

No, I don't care. (I'll probably change my mind once I see food.)

And I do change my mind. Sometimes the answer no is more positive than yes. None of us is truly hungry, just scared to see what's inside the museum. My parents both reach for coffees—my father calls it Joe—and blueberry muffins. I choose lime Jell-O with cherries of the dead floating inside. As nervous as they are, my parents eat their muffins with extreme grace, concealing any trace of inner turmoil. They are experts at peeling off the paper, splitting the top half from the bottom, then breaking it into quarters and eighths, tossing a piece into their mouths with their fingertips. They wink at each other. One of them seems to be humming; I can't tell which. When my parents argue it's hard to believe that they actually love each other. I expect one to kill the other.

Would you like a taste? My father extends a bite at me.

No, I say. Would you like some of this? I point with my spoon.

Yes, as a matter of fact, I would. It looks refreshing.

My father leans forward, hands in lap. He closes his eyes and opens his mouth. My father brushes his teeth every morning but still they are filthy and gray. I prepare a spoonful for him. He holds it in his mouth and sighs. He tries to be a boy. I don't know why my mother likes that. He even sucks his thumb. But they want me to act like a man. He lets the Jell-O break down, then gargles and jets the liquid inside his mouth. He smiles, holding the cherry between his teeth.

Is that for me? my mother asks. Her eyes brighten. She leans forward, parts her lips; she closes her eyes. My father pushes the cherry into her mouth with his tongue. Those cherries are soaked in the same stuff doctors inject into dead people. I could eat a whole jar of them.

We wipe our mouths with napkins and stand. My father takes a little extra time on his mustache. The arrows of the mustache point down and make

33

him look devilish. My parents take each other's hand and walk out of the cafeteria. I fall back behind them. I hate holding hands. They stop and wait for me, so I pass them up. Holding hands is terrible. I would like to be unknown. Not the son of anyone. Not a boy with concerned parents who make sure his shoelaces are tied tight and his underwear clean beyond belief. I want people to think I live in a trash-can with wildcats and German shepherds. If I'm the only person who knows this, that's okay; I know it's true. I say, lock an anvil to my ankle rather than walk hand in hand with an adult of any kind. I'm not craving the ALL KID PLANET. Adults are good and something to move toward but I don't want to touch them so much. They're always forc-ing me back into the baby carriage. I served my time. If I'm going to be a prisoner again, let me at least have the opportunity of killing someone first. Smashing a face off. Don't lock me up for being ten years old.

I continue straight ahead, walking up a flight of stairs wide enough to accommodate twenty people on a single step at the same time. The museum looks like a giant version of our church, with the exception of the pastel-colored banners announcing dates and peculiar names. They're proclaiming something I don't know anything about, like the obscure specials my mom is intrigued by at the supermarket. I see the ticket booth: I head for it, a tiny fancy outhouse.

Behind the glass is a person older than my parents, in a blue uniform. I reach for my wallet.

Three please. I have eleven one-dollar bills. Tickets are three dollars each. I got it covered easy.

How old are you? the lady asks.

Eleven. (What, am I too young to get in?)

Twelve and under get in free, she says.

Well then, two adults, please. Could you hurry, my parents are right behind me.

That's sweet, are you going to pay for them? She's smiling, looking over my shoulder.

By now my father and mom are standing beside me. The lady takes my father's twenty in exchange for two tickets and a pile of singles and a five.

35

THE MUSEUM DOESN'T give me the creeps. It could be a department store. My father hands the tickets to the outstretched hand of a sleepy girl. She looks like a nurse, dressed in all white with a strange angular hat on her head. To her left is a policeman. He's telling her about a lesson he taught someone. He doesn't frisk us. I got away again. He doesn't know what I've done nor what I'll do next. Sucker. He probably knows karate. He could kill my father. But I would snatch his gun and save my father. I'd say, Hold it right there, Bub, or I'll waste you. Then I'd kick him in the balls and poke out his eyes.

I'd pick up the little marbles and say, What are you looking at? You can't scare me, and then hand the dirty eyes back to him, so they could be reused, but it would never be the same. If my father fell off a cliff I would stand under his enormous flying body and brace his fall. The only thing that could crush me would be his tears. Seeing my father cry; the earth splits in two. Nothing is real; everyone's a spy; no one can be trusted; everybody whispers. Another policeman points us to the right like we're crazy clowns.

I can't believe what I'm seeing: a lion biting a naked man on the ass. A sculpture. The man is screaming but he sort of looks like he's singing. Maybe this is how he wanted to die. Maybe it's a story from the Bible. Edward, this boy at school, said he wants to die like that. He also said he'd like to swallow a grenade (his mouth isn't big enough) or have Indians shoot ninety-nine arrows into his heart. The man's about ten feet tall, with fat macaroni hair. The man and lion are all white with swirls of black. They look like the floor at the post office, frozen, like marble fudge ice cream. The man looks like the oldest muscle man in the world. He must be seventy, with giant muscles popping out everywhere and weird tiny nipples on his chest. One of the lion's paws—the animal looks human for some reason—is ripping through the man's right thigh. This is the wildest thing in the world. The man's left hand is caught in a split stump of wood. So many things are going wrong for him. As heavy as the man and beast appear they really look as though they're floating away. The man's feet are giant, bony and full of veins.

Here's another sculpture. It's of a lady and two men, all with the same modeled hair. An old bearded man is squatting, balancing his body with his right hand while the thumb of his left is jammed into his right eye. He's in agony, not from the weight of the younger man straddling him (it looks like he's making a pee-yoo gesture because the young guy's naked behind is right in his face), but rather because this young man is carrying a naked woman, and he might be jealous. Her bare chest is right above his eyes. Her mouth is open. She's screaming for help, or laughing. Her right arm is half signaling to the old man and half resisting the grip of the younger—I don't know—but her left hand is definitely reaching toward the sky. The three are twisted up like a spiral staircase.

More naked people. Three. A giant bearded man flanked by two tiny men, real shrimps. I think they're supposed to be children even though they have worried, adult faces. All have a sheet mysteriously hanging from their shoulders. A little thing suspended between each pair of legs, like a doggie turd. It's a penis and it looks like it's going to fall off. The biggest, fattest, most determined snake in the world

37

is coiling around their legs and arms. The boy-men are annoyed. The giant man is angry. Every vein and muscle in his body is popping out. His kneecaps are crazy monsters; they look like shrunken skulls. I finally found the head of the snake. It's got large, deep-set eyes. It's about to chomp into the side of the man. That's why the man is so freaked. This is a picture made out of super giant rock. It's hard to believe these sculptures were made by human hands. For the characters living inside the sculptures, this is the worst moment of their lives, and for the artist who made this, it's the best thing that ever happened.

I need to lie down. I can't look at anything else right now. Terrified, struggling, curly haired people being killed and eaten by animals. I'm frightened for them; at the same time, it's totally cool.

I've lost my parents. They must be in another room. A man is staring at me. He looks like he's about to sneeze. His nose scrunches up, but then he doesn't. He moves toward me. One of his legs is floppy and out of control but he seems completely used to it, jabbing a yellow cane into the carpet at precise intervals. He stops and begins to sneeze. Again, he stops. Maybe these aren't sneezes. He looks at me. His eyes are drawing me toward him. He delivers an unspoken message: Listen to me: I am your new owner. This place is very spooky and you should be careful—very careful. Your parents are dead. Now I will transform you into a strong leg and you will carry me through life. You will be invisible. Prepare for the de-kidding. This man is standing a foot away from me. His breathing is louder than a dishwasher. His eyes are blue. His teeth, jagged and gray. I walk away as he starts another sneeze. Maybe the creepiest man in the world.

I can go farther; I can get more lost. This next room is filled with paintings. I speed by a painting of a squashed tomato, a painting of a knife and a cut-up lemon, a lady on a swing, two people walking hand in hand down a path, a mob of carnival ghouls, winged angels in a church... My head is pounding. I feel dizzy but I feel like Max, which is who I am: Max... My insides. What am I going to do? I can't stand it. I'm going to jump out of my skin and fly away. I walk to another room. More paintings. More adults whispering and wobbling on their heels with their hands behind their backs. I run up a flight of stairs. All the paintings are black. I'm a bad guy, outlaw deluxe.

I lie down on the floor. People are extra quiet in here. The black makes them shut up. They think it's a funeral. On my belly I hear strange sounds from the carpet, an ocean of hisses and voices, rumblings of restless phantoms, and the air conditioner. I float across the surface of the floor. The feet and legs of adults pass me by.

39

I just thought of something. When I die I'll be a sculpture too: in the ground, in a box, wearing a suit and tie like I am now, with a flower on my chest, and when it rains up on the earth the drops will trickle down and get the other dead people and me all wet—but I'm sure that'll be the most refreshing drink we ever have. I know how important it is that we remain dry so we can be competent ghosts. But I'm sure a soggy ghost can do things the dry and chalky ones wouldn't think of doing. This is one reason I want to kill myself: I want to live down there, now. I also saw a man kill himself in a movie and it looked cool. Ghosts are just like people. They prefer standing over sitting, silence over talking, orange juice over milk. They have tempers. Some are swift and pretty; others are clumsy and ugly. My grandmother said she would be a ghost and to watch out for her, and now she is one. She died two years ago. She smelled bad. She didn't brush her teeth for thirty years. Sitting in the back seat with her was a huge torture. She used to sit by the fireplace and rub two holes into the carpet with her feet. And my parents wouldn't let me have a dog. I should have said, What about Grandma? Isn't she decreasing the value of the house? That would be definite grounds for a spanking.

My father makes sure his spankings hurt—that I'm crying, not laughing. To save my life I practically have to say, These are tears, Dad. I swear to

God, I'm not laughing. Look: boo hoo. That's another thing I haven't figured out: why my laughter burns him up. As a ghost my grandmother now sits across from my bed and plays the piano she brings with her. She performed concerts when she was young, and she's still a pro. She usually plays cheerful ragtime stuff. Her singing style is an eerie high-pitched gargle. Grandma, I'm sorry I called you a *dummkopf*. I did it because I liked the way it sounded on *Hogan's Heroes*. I knew it was an insult but I thought you didn't hear what people said to you. You slapped me and then told my parents and they hit me some more—so we're even and I don't have to say I'm sorry now, but I am because I miss you.

    Here's something really weird: I say I'm sorry all day long. Every night I think of things I've done wrong and the people I apologized to. My mother, my father, one of a bunch of guarded neighbors, a teacher, a schoolmate. It's dumb how much people insist on hearing the words I'm sorry. I kick someone, knock over a milk, hide a boy's lunch, throw a ball over a fence, make faces in class; I make car-crash, siren and explosion sounds; play with my spit, flick snot, karate chop pencils, give a boy a melvin (never a girl, that's forbidden—Mrs. Knight will tell the principal, Mrs. Ninnigar, and she'll call my parents; then they all get together and stare at me), eat a taco right before dinner and then I'm not hungry for mom's dinner, look under my mom's dress (seems like a good idea), throw up in bed instead of in the bathroom, pee in the garage, start fires in the alley, burn bugs, smoke cigarettes. In various combinations I do practically all these things every day.

Excuse me, sir. A policeman taps me on the shoulder. I think he's talking to me. You're not permitted to be in a prone position while visiting the museum, he says. He looks as tall as a building. He's square, another guy made out of stone. I know if I stay still for another second he'll go berserk. Boom.

Do you understand what I'm saying? he says. Are you alright?

What's a prone position? I ask.

Please stand up, young man, he says, or I'll pick you up myself. His hands are on his hips. He's tapping his foot, a shiny black shoe.

Another brush with the law. I stand up and walk through another room. To one side there's a partition with a sign that reads: DO NOT ENTER. Hmm... I'll investigate.

There's a painting of a naked girl. I think she's as old as me. Her eyes are green; she's in a green room. I love green; green's scary. She's standing in front of a thin white curtain that hovers behind her like a veil—it magically parts for her. The white flowers in the fabric look like they're eavesdropping, and the lacy fringe resembles the grasp of an octopus.

One giant pink flower peers over her right shoulder like a dragonfly; it's staring at her chest. She's pale like the marble people but she looks more like transparent wood. She has huge pink ears and blue veins running down her stomach and legs; a red bow in her brown hair, which is braided, its knotted end resting awkwardly on her left shoulder like a mangled tail. Her belly sticks out—there's a yellow ring around the button. She's scared. What's the matter? Why aren't you breathing? You're standing at attention like a soldier. I get frozen too when I'm scared. Why are your hands so dirty? Were you digging, or burying something? Are you thirsty? I could splash some water on you. Are you going to barf? I wish I could see your fingertips and the rest of your legs. You're being quiet. What would you do if I wasn't here? Take a nap? I wear pajamas when I sleep. I tuck them in. I don't want my belly touching anything. Do you want to hang out with me? I ditched my parents. They're probably asking all the policemen if they've seen me. I wonder if they'll shoot me if they catch us talking. I'll protect you. May I take you off the wall? I promise I won't hurt you. You're not heavy. That must be your Thing. You look so incredible. I've never seen one even though I know that that's it. I'll take my clothes off too; it's boiling in here. I look pretty dumb with a suit on anyway. I'll sit here and you sit there. Would you let me kiss you? Paintings

43

aren't as soft as they look. Your lips are so thick and red. You smell like a jelly doughnut. Let's be friends. I've never been friends with a girl before. You're sort of like a boy except your hair is longer and your Thing goes in. Mine goes out, see? There are weird computer words for yours and mine. Yours is *vagina*; mine is *penis*. I like saying those words. Do you like living here? I would. I like carpet and no furniture. Where I live the floors are all wood and it hurts my butt to sit long. Look, my penis is moving around— it's turning red and pointing up. I hope I'm not getting sick. I feel okay, but I kind of don't. I feel like I'm in an elevator and we're going down real fast. Can I touch you there? You can touch me if you want to. I won't go to the bathroom. I know you bleed there. Does that scare you? How did you get so smart? I like blood. Could I put it in you? You feel slippery. I wonder if this is how you... I've watched my parents but I couldn't see exactly what they were doing. Do you leave it in for a while? This is wicked. I wonder why I like you so much. It feels like I'm being electrocuted in a good way. I feel like I'm flying. I'm dizzy. Are you dizzy? You're so funny. Please kiss me again. Thank you. I guess I'll put my clothes on now. I don't want to go but I think I better. Maybe I can take you home with me. I could stick you in my jacket but I don't think you'll fit. I can't believe you'd like a boy like me. Where's my other sock? I hate underwear.

My mom makes me wear T-shirts so I won't catch cold. Do you want to smell my shoes? They stink bad. You seem more real to me than the girls at school. They huddle in a circle and vote on who's the cutest. They point at boys and pretend they're dying. They laugh in mean ways. I know they're probably nice but they hide it. You told me what scares you. You let me mess you up. You told me why being a girl makes you fierce and shy. I sort of feel like that too. I wish I were as much of an animal as you.

Flesh Is for Hacking

FAVORITE PARTS—I save them, I love them (torso, head). I throw the rest away (feet, legs, arms); I hate them (toes, too). But I love elbows. It's unsettling how elbows are pointy one minute and squishy and flaccid the next. No different than myself, or any man for that matter. I pinch my own elbow when I feel tense. I do it all day long.

A person never truly appreciates a head until they see it separated, by itself, on a stick, or held in your hands. You nuzzle it. You twist the ear and no one shouts. A thing that once screamed so loud is now a perfection in pieces, my silent ecstasy.

I address the head. I start an argument, lose my patience and sling it across the room. The head thumps against the wall and plops to the ground in a mute sort of way, more like a sandbag. Human flesh hitting a hardwood floor is a recognizable sound. I'd call it classical.

This morning, at a cost of twenty-four dollars (marked down from twenty-nine), I purchased a red valise. Is that an obvious color? The head and torso fit neatly inside. I've never gotten over the fact that vinyl is such a superior material. Inexpensive, looks like leather and any stain wipes right off.

I close the lid. My joy is gone. It disappears the way the world blackens when I shut my eyes—so quick and cold. The fuzzy shapes remain in my warm brain. With my nasal congestion I'm unable to smell what I trust to be supremely aromatic: the decomposing boy.

Wednesday nights are trash nights. Skunks come down from the mountains and waddle through the neighborhood garbage. That's my second favorite smell: skunks. They're so wonderful, so slow and vulnerable. Doesn't that make sense in a funny way, a stinky animal picks at stinky food? For the record— since I'm here to tell all—other unpopular smells close in the running: cheese, gasoline, sulphur, my arm pits, my farts. When I fart (my farts are brilliant) I see a stranger in my basement. He is moaning but not unhappy.

I OPEN THE VALISE. The boy is still with me. God bless him, even if he wasn't a good boy. God bless me. I know better.

I lift the head from the valise. By itself it weighs as much as a small baby. You are so much trouble. I step out of my underwear and play with the head. I bounce it against my pimply butt: *boing boing*. I've never been able to keep my butt free of blemishes. I feel silly applying teenage medicine back there at my age, but I do it anyway. I make the effort. I plant the boy's face up my ass, his naughty little pug nose Eskimo kisses my buggy hole. I try to fart. Nothing. I feel a shit inside but unfortunately it's too far up to come out.

From the mirror on the wall I can tell you that my asshole looks just like anyone else's. Shall we say, like a corrupt bellybutton? No better, no worse. It's just there, puckered and inscrutable. And that means I'm here, living and breathing. Some people pinch themselves. It's a good thing to do. Check and see if you're still here. If I'm still here.

I bring the head around to my belly and rub my cock against the bridge of his nose. Such patience. Thank you. I push myself into his stubborn mouth and fuck the gray face. I need a new watchband. I've had this one six months. They should last longer than that. I pull out all the way, to see myself—hello there—and then all the way back in. That's what it's all about... as deep as I can. I twirl the head around like a slow pinwheel. When was the last time he brushed those teeth? I know it's been at least two days. Teeth feel good. I like it when it hurts. Yes, yes, just like that. Uh huh. Oh, you little fuckhead, you dead little shit. My God, you can't do this to me. And when I've suffered as much pain as I can stand I pull out and squirt on your eyelids.

Killing, cutting up boys has made me a better person. It took me so long to notice. For instance, now I give without expecting something in return.

Ardmore

I WAS OVER BY THE clothesline, hanging a few things out to dry. A strange man startled me. He was hiding behind a machine that looked a little too much like a weapon, a small cannon or something, with a very fat glass barrel and long wooden legs. It made a windy sound like a vacuum cleaner, as if it were going to fly toward me and bite. My heart dropped and my knees buckled.

My husband, Crease, peeked his head out from under the house to see what was up, his face covered with unmentionable filth. The stranger aimed the machine at my husband; he pointed it at our car that we've yet to repair. Then it hit me and I felt like blushing. The contraption wasn't no gun but a fancy motion picture camera. And the stranger, of course, was shooting a movie. He walked out from behind the camera and introduced himself. He said we captured the despair of this region and would I mind repeating what I'd just done: unpin the laundry, toss it back in the bucket, then hang it all up again. I made a quarter turn and spat at a tree and pretended I didn't hear that.

Dad was rocking on the porch, whittling another giraffe. He has the wood between his legs, the tiny head atop the long neck, the two bulging eyes and two darling gnarled ears. When he finishes cutting and polishing his carvings he places them on the ledge above the fireplace where his kingdom resides. My six kids were scampering around the yard, screaming their lungs out.

The stranger took pictures of everything. I felt like my life was a plate of food and he was scarfing it up. The stranger had partners, two other men with cameras on legs. They were busy with the sky, trees and pond.

These people, they weren't from around here. Their cars had out-of-state plates and their clothes looked brand new. They walked around the property like nervous policemen. They were quick and stiff and called me ma'am. Their faces were scrubbed clean, no beards, their teeth bright and shiny. The man's request for me to work twice as much was plain silly, though his little army stood friendly enough. Anyway, I thought it best to go inform Ardmore that

51

something was up, that strangers with cameras were taking pictures on his land. If someone breaks the sugar bowl I want to hear about it immediately. I don't want to grab the thing and have it fall apart in my hands. I slipped away across the ravine to convey what was going on to Ardmore. I could use a break. My hands were soggy, they needed to dry out, and I felt like a stroll.

Ardmore built all these houses around here, as well as a special one he never moved into. He built this house for himself and a spouse—hammered the nails, planed the corners, but Ardmore's remained womanless. He filled the house with furniture but left it in boxes. I don't joke with him about whether the warranties are still good.

Ardmore's surliness makes it unlikely any female will ever kiss his cheek, boil his coffee or bury his soul. Ardmore believes the earth owes him a woman for his life of tolerance. I'd like to know what sort of reward the world gets for tolerating Ardmore. I should talk. I have a bad temper, I talk loudly to myself when I work, my feet are ugly, especially the baby toes (at least I got them), I frequently burn supper and kill hours off Crease's sleep time, and possibly his life, with my snoring. At age seventy-one Ardmore continues to wait for marriage with a tightly shut jaw, folded arms and swollen feet. I've seen them soaking. When he stops by for the rent, I pour him a lemon-ade and strongly doubt he'll ever cross the threshold.

Ardmore exploded just as I expected. His pink face turned a darker, wilder red. He screamed and spit and took off back to our place like a weak bullet. I followed. I got excited in that worried way. I hate violence but I'd rather see it and then push it away from me rather than never get a decent look at it.

As we walked up, the camera folk were packing everything away, laughing, talking technical. Ardmore shouted for them all to get off his property, that they had no business kicking up their heels at his expense. No one's going to treat honest country folk like pharmaceutical monkeys. Ardmore wanted them to disappear now but they weren't moving nearly fast enough.

Ardmore pulled that gun of his out from a coat pocket and shot twice but didn't hit anything. One of the camera boys muttered that the old geezer was shooting blanks. With that, Ardmore planted both feet real careful and shot the boy in the chest. The bullet turned him into a man—a dead one. He looked at Ardmore, stunned and unhappy, like he'd never been shot before. He said, You didn't have to do that. The blood seeped through his clean shirt, a real nice plaid, before leaking out of his mouth. He smiled, or winced, and with both hands covered the spot where the bullet went in. Blood spilled over his bottom lip and marked his chin. He teetered. Whatever he was holding dropped, then he wiggled

53

to the ground. Ardmore continued hollering for them all to go, to move faster. Who wanted to be next, he said.

We all just stood there, quietly breathing, keeping our eyes half on Ardmore and half on one of the chickens that had burst on the scene as if suddenly craving to be tonight's main course. All of us were a little wounded and dazed. Without looking I knew Ardmore's eyes resembled tiny erasers. I stared at his feet. They were turned out like a duck's.

Now, Ardmore's fuse is pretty short, but I wouldn't say it's shorter than anyone else's around here. It's our insides, and it's not changing.

I had failed to mention to Ardmore, besides the fact that the camera people were suspicious with their out-of-state plates and all, that they were basically nice. So nice, in fact, they paid us a month's rent for the inconvenience. The money belongs to my family. We pay the rent.

I've been thinking about this through the night and into the morning. I roll it over and over and a funny feeling strikes me, a bad one—possibly what guilt feels like. It tickles and pulls, makes me sick. I believe Ardmore was right in shooting and I did the correct thing in providing him with the information. The only way to stop people from taking advantage of you is to stop them cold. Everyone knows that. Otherwise you're steamrolled like a pancake and you're crying, Why me? Sure it's questionable how much we were being took. Maybe not at all. That's what makes me feel this way. So much confusion. I think the problem I'm having has to do with being the center of attention. I liked being filmed and I desperately want to see what I look like.

Real Me

THERE'S A GAME to be played, to be taken seriously, a special game that happens on a big night when everything's quiet and still. That's how I think of it. It shoots the nerves way up, gets me breathing fast, rushes me home an hour early from work. It's so demanding. It's so fun. It's so bad, wacky, low.

A puff on a cigarette. God this room is great. What *was* the architect thinking? I live in what appears to be an upside-down bread loaf pan. *Drown yourself.*

Warm tonight. This is my last cigarette. Puff. Out. Maybe some champagne. Later perhaps, at the height of it all. No no no, right now. I *must* taste bubbly this instant. A brilliant man always keeps a bottle chilled in the fridge for gloom, intrigue and celebration. One never knows.

A toast. Here's to a pitiful man who enjoyed himself in spite of two million shortcomings. We... *love you.*

Thank you very much. You're all very sweet. Now stop looking at me. Enjoy yourselves, I'll be right back.

Stay with us. Don't go.

Must go. Urgent.

Step into my office, grab scissors; waltz right into the little gameroom, the bathroom. A look in the mirror. You're a man. Not bad. Thank you. You're welcome. Off with my pants, off off off. Look, there's a penis down there. Who's going to eat it? Someone with a huge appetite, I guess. We cut the crotch away from the underwear, pull the fabric down over the hips: now it's a skirt. You're a hula dancer. Dance, boy. Hairy...little...balls...sag for attention. Me me me. Won't someone tickle me? You in the back row, shut up.

So cruel.

We pull the two boys out for a good scratch. Poor things. They're so forlorn. I love you. Good-bye now.

Thanks, Mister.

We rub lipstick on the mouth, so succulent; slip hoops through the earlobes; glue eyelashes on the eyes; a little mascara, couple dabs of rouge; strap the bra around the chest.

Awfully pretty.

Take out the lasso.

57

(Theatrical, aloof.) You know, Cummerbund, you look *so* handsome tonight, but I'm afraid I'm just too pooped to go out. (Yawns.) You'll have to stalk the world of pork chops alone if your cabin fever is as bad as it sounds.

(Jams hands in pockets, peeved.) Is that so? I think you take the homebody thing too far. I think you're cheating on me.

Don't be silly. (Dismisses with hand wave.) I love you. You're my hammer and anvil. All creatures pale in comparison. You're *it* in my book. (Dips index finger onto tongue, draws letters *I T* in the air.)

(Folds arms across chest.) I bet you have some side order outside right now waiting for you to flash the lights three times.

(Three-quarter look, hands on hips.) Why are you thinking these things? Stop being a grumpy buffalo. (Straightens up, grabs hold of neck.) What are you doing? (Squeezes lightly.) That hurts. (Struggle.) Let go of me. (Lasso around neck.) What are you doing? Are you completely crackers? (Sticks out tongue.)

Oh, my little stink boy, I'm sorry. Did I guess the secret code? Is the plumber or the Fuller Brush man on his way up? (Tightens rope, soft punch to face.) Looks like we're going to have quite a scene now.

(Continues to struggle.) Shut up.

(Pushes against wall opposite mirror.) No, you shut up. (Solid punch to face.) You're a sneak, a trickster, an evil swine.

(Frightened, disoriented.) Ouch. That really hurt. You're paranoid. (Lifts end of rope up to mouth, smears lipstick.) Quit it. What are you doing with the lasso? You're ruining my mouth. Let me go. (Slips rope over head, tightens around neck.) Stop it. I can't breathe. (Coughs, sticks out tongue.)

You look stupid. And very old. Close your mouth when you're dying. (Stomps twice on the floor.) And now the knock at the door. All these surprises. (Hand on chin, in mock query.) Gee, I wonder who that is? (Tightens rope.)

Stop choking me, I'm serious. (Gags.) I can't... breathe.

(Pleased with himself.) Thought you could push little old me out the door for a couple hours while you have a carnal tryst with a strapping young colt. (Punches in the stomach.) Sorry to spoil all the fun, (punches again) but you're a dead cunt with a boring cock. (Bangs face against mirror.)

(Flails, spits.) Please, please stop. Answer the door. I'm sure it's only Milton. I really can't breathe. You're going to kill me. (In tears.) I love you. You (sings song) *and nobody else but you.* You've got to believe me.

You're nauseating me. I'm going to kill you. (Punches in the face. Tightens rope all the way, and pulls; slams head against back wall.) You shouldn't live another second. (Slam.) You're too old. You're a wrinkled slimy pile of shit. (Stuffs rag in mouth.) I hate your tongue, so fat and smelly; (slam) I hate the sounds it makes. (Slam.) You're gone. I'm out of here. (Slam.)

(Inaudible) Don't leave me.

Pubic Hair

MY SEX IS NOT important. I believe this could happen to anyone in the world, anyone with hair on their body. No, I am not speaking from personal experience (yes I am) nor have I been told this by a friend (I will receive the amusing comeback, "You have no friends"). Nor (I have pointed this out many times in the past) am I particularly hairy. Nor am I hiding behind the pretense that a so-called client told me this. I am employed but I make very little money. I don't work *with* people, I work *at* them, so the words client and associate are inappropriate to me. This is simply information. It is also a true story—which is why I beat around the bush— and as I stated at the outset, this could happen to anyone, and for that reason hear me out. In the porn films I've seen, the individuals are discreet about removing pubic hairs from their mouths, but for some reason my companion in real life, the focal point of all my teeth-gritting oceanic barnyard thoughts, has gotten into the habit of spitting my pubic hair out while still down at x doing the oral nasty. I should be infinitely grateful that I'm even paired up with another human creature (true), the world's a lonely place, and the blessed fact that the creature is so skilled at the lick-slurp-gnaw (truer still), but more so that they are even willing to face-battle in the first place—Oh, how I can feel for the league of the sexually neglected (I can't help gloating) and see their watery eyes and shaky hands drift toward their circles or their sticks and then pull quickly away. What is the point? To not give or not be given head/mouth and teeth–love is to be plunged into the disturbing maelstrom of loin loss, which is to say that spitting out my pubic hair isn't as bad as some things but it is extremely disconcerting and sets the sexual climb back to square one, or, to be honest, throws it into an unfortunate pothole. If my pubic hairs were to be used as dental floss or ingested as a munchy little salad, that would also be cause for sadness. An argument could be made that spitting is a physically economic move. Why stop the industrious hand that wanders across my chest or digs deep to squeeze life (that was never there) into my butt to take care of the dead and banal business of picking pubic hair out of one's teeth. There is the act of spitting itself, to one side or the other, never directly in my face, thank God. It lands on other parts of the bed and often drizzles my legs. Most troublesome is the sound. People spit into gutters. Baseball players spit tobacco to relax, to remind themselves that they are men, to say I am outdoors, this is work, I'm an animal, I fear no one. Yours truly has never been a successful spitter. When I try it, saliva clings above and below my lips and usually finds its way on to my clothes. The real problem about all this is not the act of spitting but how spitting brings to mind my nervousness about my crotch area, about having a sex organ in the first place—a stick or a circle—and maintaining its appearance (keeping it pleasant). No one wants the bush in and of itself, a dense patch of bonsai fur, in their mouth, period. I understand. Do I shave it off and continue to keep the area smooth (that could keep me young) until sex has terminated *in my life?* That's a legitimate question and I will remember that. I will. Spitting is an impulse and saliva is one of the many fluids of affection. It happens every single time, within fifteen seconds. First a hesitation, a head turn, and then *thpoow!* After that, after things get wet, or once the experience overtakes my partner, they can't tell if there's another pubic hair in their mouth, because they've lost control. And that's a good thing, and why this is not such a terrible problem. I am privileged to breathe air for lungs and brain and speak words at all. I believe it was Darwin who said, "When the head is good the heart will pump." I

63

scratch quill to onionskin for the sole purpose of human understanding. Please accept my apologies. I can't help but sound like the world is coming to an end. I was born into the doomsday mindset. I am *not* proud of my pubic hair and frankly I don't see how a person *can* be proud of pubic hair. Even when it's blond or red it's still mangy—actually more so, the way it blends into the flesh. But there is still something endearing about pubic hair when thought of or seen in the proper light. If I received a pubic hair in the mail, taped to a love letter for instance, even from the above mentioned individual who, as I plainly stated earlier, spits them out, I would be overcome with excitement, and possibly a little frightened. But that's one pubic hair (in a world where trillions sprout and curl) pulled from the root, isolated on a sheet of paper (not spat from someone's mouth like gristle). In magazines featuring naked men and women all the rash-free crotches feature pubic hair as discreetly as parsley, and with the men the gnarly bush seems to disappear with the presence of a freestanding cock. My predicament is now out in the open. And to close I will say this: if I have made a house, or a home, out of pubic hair, I'm sorry you had to enter it.

See the Way I Think

TWO FOXY FIFTH GRADERS, Liz and Connie: they wear tons of makeup and tight jeans; *dee-dee, dee dee dee*. I play guitar. It's around my neck. *Thwang...wa wa wa*. I'm going to fuck them both whether they like it or not. Tap my cock on the table of justice: But Your Honor, I was only trying to tease her, *dwang*, serenade them with my voltage. Overruled in the world sex courtroom. Juggle them on and off the cyclops, spin them around, throw them across the street. See you in homeroom; two tardies are as good as an absence. Liz and Connie, they're always looking at me; sex eyeballs, targets of intrigue. Draw a diagram of all the balls involved here: my sack-olas and their bugging bloodshots; a total of six; two of mine versus four of theirs, so you know what

I'm up against. All these balls work in pairs: their
wanton shifty eyes (sex experts, we'll see) and my
blind hanging clankers (the total pro, proven); a net
sum of three sets. I have eyes, too, I forgot, which
now makes a balanced relationship. But Liz and
Connie blur my lower and upper sets into one mass, a
single cell, and I do theirs, too, all eyes and holes into
a tight singular unit. The final picture should read,
one to one. Bring that into math class, settle that
probability. The crowd I hang out with considers me
an old man. They call me Gramps (I got a nervous
left hand, it shakes for some reason, doesn't affect my
playing); they call me the General, the King, Killer
Bee (my solos are vicious). I can spit thirty feet. I
groan, squint, rub my head a lot, walk with a limp
(motorcycle wreck). They think I'm out of my mind,
which is crucial; all that means is that I'm full of
myself in an indescribable way, like a great candy bar.
I stare people down. Then they respect me, because
I'm scary. I'll do anything. Very important. I've
jumped through windows; drove this dude's car with
no tires fifty miles an hour in reverse and then
pushed it off a cliff; won a hundred dollars for eating
ten hamburgers in five minutes (actually jammed
three in my shirt when no one was looking); head-
butted the manager of 7-11 for not selling me beer;
pounded a guy's face to a pulp at the beach with a
good-sized boulder, for calling my friends geeks; set
some decent fires; saved a baby in a fire I didn't set

(declined interviews with reporters); leapt off the roof of a friend's house, threw a brick at the school narc, pissed on the nurse's desk, pulled an earring out of the music teacher for calling my music trash, branded a kid like a rancher does a cow (bought the branding iron at the Rose Bowl swap meet for fifty cents, Circle K). So I follow the little women home after school on my bike (nobby tires, low handlebars, very cool). My hair's not perfect but I can go on living. When I have a car I will destroy life as we know it. I will recreate it in my own image, whatever that is. A gladiator. A mud pie. A weeping willow. Liz and Connie keep turning around, the frauleins, they're giggling. I'm a comedian who says nothing. The audience laughs because they don't know what else to do. I'm robo-slaughter and I got the women laughing. I'm thinking, pounce on their meat, suck their faces, rub their pussies, one in each hand. Get the squeal going. Tidal wave. Color them milky. Chug chug. I know what I want to do to them and they know I'm man enough to do it, because everyone at school knows I've done it a lot—fucked women, tiny shits as young as them and babes older than my mom. I fuck old women because they know what they're doing. They see my cock and jump for joy. They go straight for it like a diver, and they stay down, never come up for air. They play games with it (bash the lips, look no hands); they make crazy slurping sounds. Old women like it rough. Pound me, they say, pound me, Bobby. They groan and grip my ass. They go into long spastic convulsions. They're desperate for the oily *O*. Another time an older woman said, Tear it up, come on now, tear me up. We get on all fours and I tug on the lady's hair, she says, Yes, yes. She had a southern accent. That was ultracool. To them sex is better than money. I don't even have to pinch it. They hand over the twenties and tens. They want to die, I think; at least they act that way. It's weird. Why kill anyone who wants to die? Then if you blow it you've let them down. Kill people who resist it; so it stays your own gig. Little girls are different. They scream, they're fascinated. They try hard to act mature. They smooch their lipstick all over it and then start blushing. They say, It's growing. It's turning left, and giggle some more. You tell them to suck deeper and they act insulted as if that's not the procedure. Having a demon that's not sucked all the way is like sleeping with a blanket that doesn't cover your feet. Liz and Connie are the sexiest girls in school because they have the best faces; they're also intensely stupid. That's also sexy in a strange sort of way. They finish every sentence with the words *like* and *stuff*. Everything is so blurry and confusing to them. They think what we're going to do is sophisticated. They're showing off, trying to act glamorous, calling each other brat. They want to prove who's the most experienced and cool, who can suck a cock and not look retarded, which is impossible. I've done it a lot of different ways, backwards, upside down, even with a cigarette in my mouth. So Liz and Connie invite me into the happy house, Connie's parents' green and yellow apartment two blocks from school; a super fuck palace, with the sunlight busting through curtain cracks. A harsh daylight fuck. The truth of summer. A climb up my tree. Discover and appreciate the root system, the veins of my existence. Cover up for a megasplash. *Do-do do, do-do do, do do, dwang, dwang.* But they get scared when I tell them to strip, like it's done another way. They laugh and tell me to strip first. I pick up a baseball bat that's by the door and say I'll hit a few fly balls before they see my butt hairs. They laugh more. So I bash them each on the shin to let them know I mean business. Business in the sense of, I got the rod that provokes civilization, the thing, the creep, the goon, the one-eyed dog that took Eve downtown. In a fake cop voice I say, You got ears, you know what I'm talking about. Make the decision of your life. It's do as I say. It's *strip, dumb fucks.* They're both in uniform: tight torn-up blue jeans with black tights underneath. Off with everything. They obey like soldiers. They cry and strip (now it's baby time) and lie down on the carpet by the fireplace. It's not romantic anymore. There's something I want to try. I get on my knees, I start with Connie, it's her house. I stick it in her—the bat, not my killer meat. I'm warming up and Liz starts screaming again, then Connie joins in. The total

69

whiny noise pit. The bat doesn't fit very well but it looks cool. I tell them to shut their traps or they're going to end up in center field, but they don't quit, so I jump up and hit homers on their heads. They ooze like leaky eggs. I kiss them, pull down my pants, get on top of the now gooey Liz (might as well, the General is at attention). Sir, yes sir, then a messed-up Connie. Next day, police ask my parents if I'm home, and for a change I am, taking a rare break from the complex world of field research. Nothing like empirical evidence. Facts, they're wicked, and they shed light. The police take me away. My parents didn't even argue with them. They are worthless, not what I would describe as compatriots; not soul, blood or spit brothers; nothing but measly *parents*. I don't give a shit, I say fuck you a million times a day. This is how they treat the best: they stop them early. The wild ones in history act like me. The berserk brothers. I talk sense down at the station. I continue to say, in my best English, the words that brought purpose to my life: fuck you horse meat, fuck you, fuck you, fuck you, fuck you. I say it slow, I say it fast. It might be a cliché, but it means everything down here. With each usage a subtle nuance is born. They say to me, as if they're Coach Walters telling me to run laps, No way little rat, we're trying you as an adult; because of the severity of this crime, you're going to get life, little rat, life. No more listening to that moron. I get the last word. This is my story. Life is right here. Life is my face, and my eyes. Actually, I see things in reverse with patches of blackness. Let me explain. On that gloomy night fifteen years ago, Dr. Zall switched my eyes when my mom let me loose, left eye for right eye. Dr. Zall dropped them on the floor and no one cleaned them off. I remembered the doctor's name. Alien zombies of the world, the friends of my parents, with their maniac names: Slosh, Zurzur, Bliss. My dad's got a bad eye too now. He talks like a scientist. Now he's on my side (mom too) and prays I'm not guilty. He pats me on the shoulder and says, We all overreact sometimes. I ask him what's wrong with the eye; it's pink and leaky. He says, when drainage of the aqueous humor is obstructed, pressure eventually damages nerves; hence my unusual appearance. It'll be fine by the trial date, son. It's not uncommon for a man of my age. That's kind of you to ask. I close my eyes for a second. I can't point myself in a direction that doesn't make me sick. I think about the days when I was afraid to touch girls. I'd sit across the room from them, frozen. I thought all I had to do was stare and something would happen. The girl would crawl into my clothes and we'd be fucking. But they just sat there bored and wondered what was wrong with me. They'd look away; their mom would be returning from work soon. They were looking for animals. Well, I was shy then. That should've count-ed for something but it didn't pay off at the crucial moment. Shyness might have a power but it doesn't

71

get you naked. I also think about humongous peanut-eating elephants stomping on babies in the zoo because they're so big they don't even know what they're crushing; or the lions and tigers chasing down and ripping up anything that moves, especially zebras and antelope as well as more babies who accidentally wander into their cages. Final words: Get out the guitar. This is for all the rejects out there. No, seriously, I'm thinking of Mrs. Franchise, the four-foot-tall Spanish teacher. Last year she wrote a note to my mom that said, Where is the old Bobby? I miss him. We all do. Let's find him and bring him back. *Ding ding, wa wa wa*, pretty surreal. My mom showed me the note. I want to know, too, she blinks and smiles like a ghoul, where is the old you? Let's be logical here, no one panic. I think it's safe to say that the old me will never return; he's been devoured by the new.

Please

MAYBE IT WAS a chili dog. No offense, I'm not complaining, I don't do that sort of thing (complain), I don't, sets you back, sets me back. Ask anyone and they'll tell you chili dogs are my favorite main course here. I have plans and I must tell you about them since that is required of me, but first I'd like to tell you about my stomach, which nearly exploded, and as I stated above I'm afraid it was something I ate, which is nothing to be ashamed of. It was an average agony, the kind of terrible pain I'm very familiar with. I rubbed my belly and pinched the flab (a new pain often subtracts from the old) and waited for it all to pass. The ceiling caught my attention so I got up on my legs (I stood). Spiders were up there, two of them, but they vanished into the plaster.

I could do that. But when you do, will you return a different sex? How about a drink of water? I stepped into the hallway and it hit me. My legs stiffened. I could feel the Lord Jesus Christ paying very close attention to me. Get to the bathroom, he mumbled. I shivered, and felt squeezed inside out. A steel rod shot through me. I reared on my heels. My sphincter contracted like the demonic muscle it is. I wobbled into the lavatory, petrified, not breathing (I had air inside me but I couldn't use it). I was about to die. The toilet. I pulled my pants down, squatted and allowed the malicious rebellion to blast out of me (rocket that I am). My stomach problem, now simple and brown in its morbidity, vanished upon flushing. I smiled and laughed a little bit—at the things I love, mishaps, how I can't see around corners. This happens to me all the time. I try my best. It's frightening. Most folks feel warned well in advance by internal signals letting them know a movement is queuing up. Not me. Let me start with this longing I feel. I call it a hole because I imagine it looks like one. Round. Not especially deep. Let me start again. I'm requesting permission to step outside for a short while (to see some things), say twelve hours. Six in the morning to six at night. Is that excessive? Departures are best in the morning (the honest time) and I will return to this noble spot where you care for me, in time for dinner. Chili dogs, I hope. You see, I'm scared I'll never smell fresh-cut grass again, nor smell the wood at the lumberyard. I know I sound romantic but isn't everyone? Manure, clorine and all kinds of flowers. The trees that smell like semen. And gasoline, such a compelling scent. When I was a boy my mother slipped and fell at a Mobil station. She didn't have a chance to clean up. We'd been driving all day and we were in the biggest hurry to get home. For the rest of the day she smelled of gasoline. It made her cry but I loved it. Wear that stink like she did is what I think. I'm not going to kill myself. The thought never crossed my mind. It wraps around more like a circle. Round and round. On this proposed outing I'll be walking: no running (I know that's bad), no nothing—just good clean left and right stepping. I will glide from here to there. This is a perfect situation for a fellow like myself, who's in between things, to weep. I cry when I see people next to each other being nice. Wildly sentimental, that's me—highly lacking in jealousy. I'm happy for these people who don't assault each other. I commend their self-control. There's too much slaughter already. That's a commonly held belief. I wipe all tears and mucus on my shirt sleeve, and the glistening streaks along my arms let me know where I rank in the gloomy division. A five-star moper. I think more about the saliva in my mouth—how I must swallow rather than spit spit spit—than I do about my future. I do know I want to feel human and I know how ambitious that is, and how indistinct. So maybe that's

75

my goal. Human indistinction. No. I will say that no one will be with me. I will say that this is work and I need to be alone. I must concentrate. I need privacy. You don't get much of that around here. This is why I need your permission. I've been placed on earth to walk and think, not to be escorted about by people who encourage my every weakness (which you and this generous facility have catalogued). I look at my face sometimes and I think, am I a mushroom? It's a terrible face. Of so little value. The cook told me that a mushroom has no nutritional value. That shocked me. All my life I thought of the mushroom as a reining vegetable. People don't let me cry. They insist I stop. So I stop. Crying's not my goal (if there was any confusion there). I'll be alone, and if you gave me six months out there I'm fairly certain I could find a person to link up with, but not in twelve hours. I would hang around a lively lunch counter and introduce myself (as a bachelor) to an interesting person whose eyes beckon me forth. I'd pick up the routines. I hope this isn't important, me being with another person. You see, people run both ways with me in the love/hate category. My goal is to fill my little hole. To move my legs in an unrestricted area, to get floppy, to become less confused about simple things, to remember my first birthday party (I did have one, parents are scrupulous about the first one), how much icing I smeared on my face. Photographs. If I were presented with a day pass, it, the sacred slip, would be folded

by me and neatly jammed into my front pocket. I
know how vulnerable back pockets can be. I know
how things get squished, then slide, scoot and flip-
flop down the alley. Every step I take you know I do
with the understanding that it's a privilege and that
I've been trusted to be responsible (even if nobody
trusts me). I respect that. If my head spins off (and I
don't see why it should) I'd better make sure my head
doesn't sail in the street and distract a funeral procession or a hot-rodder into a pileup. If I take my
clothes off I promise to fold them flat (like I've been
taught) so another man or woman may wear them. I
guess I've revealed an additional interest: taking off
my clothes. I feel friendlier naked. This is tied into   77
the freshly cut grass. I want to rub my ass and elbows
and belly on cool prickly grass. I will not eat any
because I know my stomach is temperamental. Mild
things can be so dangerous. But I will take a snooze
and dream about animals (polar bear, otter, monkey,
mongoose). My goal is to return smiling and I will
achieve this glowing posture by being prompt and
keeping my antennae up to receive all peripheral
data, and I'll breathe. I get a lot out of breathing. For
me that's often more than enough. I will touch things
I love and be wary and considerate of objectionable
objects; also try and touch coarse things. Wood. I
love wood. I press my cheek to it and roll my face
over its surface. I pucker up for a little kiss. I try not
to drool. I know moisture is harmful. A warped plank

is a sorry sight. I'll be cautious and polite. I just don't want to get a splinter. When I was nine years old I got a splinter in my pinky and my father came at me with a burning needle and said he was going to put an end to my accident. I dove out the window and the next thing I knew I was eating Jell-O through a straw. I can't emphasize enough how dangerous a splinter can be. Other problems I'll encounter? Too numerous to mention but I'll be blunt: they're there. I'll throw out a couple of potential hazards. A large bird decides to follow me. It circles over my head, waiting for me to fall down and die so it can eat. Your basic survival-of-the-fittest situation. The bird gets hungrier as I continue to stand, resisting death. I walk merrily down the street. My courage is noticeable. The bird shoots a bowel movement toward my head. I dodge the powerful turd. If the white blob landed in my eye he would have me. He could peck me apart as I struggled to regain my vision. The bird, corrupt to the core, desperate and angry, swoops down and attacks me regardless of my advantages. A pinch with its claws, a peck from the beak is as much as I will allow. I seize the bird by the throat and squeeze the life out, just like that. I'm not a military man but I do believe in defending oneself. With certain subjects I have the strength of a cartoon character. I hope you know this is true with all men and women—the hidden powers. I'm not saying that we're all gods, or that I aspire to be one, just that we're occasionally specialists. But what happens when a gang of newborn babies break away from their mother's breasts and try to eat me with their toothless mouths? This is another problem. No, I wouldn't grab them by their feet and sling the doughy bodies against the wall. I'd whisper stories to them—things their parents neglected to tell them, like the bus driver's conflict and the trash collector's awakening, or the roofer's freak show. I aim to please. I go straight to the grocery store and buy a pack of bubble gum and blow big ones until my jaws are weak. I predict a spotless voyage as if I were a spotless lamb. I have kept it a secret. No one on the planet knows. No one living. There are spirits who know but they keep their traps shut. Be a pal to a spirit and you'll experience dedication like you've never known. I'm talking hard-core loyalty. When the walls sweat cold coffee (which happens) the spirits assure me there's nothing to worry about. Secrets get big inside me; I could die if I'm not careful (from the pressure and all). But I don't explode. It's amazing how durable a man's elastic is. A spirit cools me off with a blow of air. I'll write my name a thousand times if you want me to, if it's the only way you'll believe me. Every time I'm in a group I shout to myself the titles of famous books and their famous opening sentences. Doing this fortifies me and renders me invisible or armless and part of the group. I feel armless when I arrange my arms uniformly at my sides. Blending in is my mainstay. I'll wear earth

79

tones or all blue, depending on the group's feelings. Yellow and orange in the summer. I think I'm professional in groups. Everyone here wears white but I know none of you are saints. I pretend I'm a little sad so as not to appear too happy. I wish the best for my neighbors and their families. I'll take off my clothes if someone is cold. I'll give them my hair if they're crying about being bald. My father is bald and he loves it. He still combs his hair. He combs nothing and when he brushes his teeth and shaves he practices faces for a circus act he's never performed. But it's true, there's no limit to how responsible I can be. I take all my pills at the right time. I love them as I do a friend. I wouldn't let a pill down. I am my pills (if I may say so) and I never miss a television program. I consider this a feature quality in my arsenal of love. *Bullwinkle* is on at 6:00 A.M. At 5:45 I'm warming up the set. I've already gone to the bathroom and I will not touch my milk until I see his antlers.

Truants

A TRUANT OFFICER who wore a badge and black hat discovered three boys swimming in a public pool. He recognized the boys from school but he did not know their names. He fancied himself a man who took bad things and yanked them inside out. Bad is easily changed to good, he'd say at assembly; I'm hardly ever wrong. His hands were large and scary. They looked like slabs of raw pork. The three brothers splashed around in the pool. Every time one of them did something, like a backflip or a bellyflop or a cannonball, he'd scream for the attention of the other two. Using his extra-long left arm the truant officer reached across the water and pulled the closest boy out. He dropped him into a thirty-gallon gunny sack. He fished out the second boy, who was holding his breath at the bottom of the deep end, by slipping a long stick through the leg of his shorts. He was tossed into the sack. With the aid of a crossbow the truant officer launched a plunger at the third truant, catching him on the buttocks and reeling him in like a fish. He was also dropped into the sack. The truant officer tied the neck of the sack into an elaborate knot and stormed toward school.

With their toes and elbows poking into each other's kidneys and armpits and eyesockets the brothers escaped suffocation by enlarging a tiny hole at the bottom of the burlap sack. Once the hole was as large as their heads they slid out of the bag and ran for their lives. They made it to their fort just ahead of the truant officer, who shouted vulgar phrases at them. The brothers banged into each other saying, What do we do now? T.O.'s going to kill us. The truant officer was out of breath and wanted to kill the boys, or at least one and have the others watch in horror. How else would they learn their lesson? Bayoneting Krauts: the truant officer killed dozens of unarmed soldiers during the big war. He was not proud of that and could never shake the memory of warm blood squirting back onto his cheeks and into his eyes.

Signs plastered on all four sides of the fort begged the world to stay away: SCRAM. NO ADULTS. BEWARE. DEATH TO THOSE WHO TRY. The truant officer ignored them and pounded on the door. He was standing on their skull-and-crossbones doormat.

From inside the fort they pulled the rug out from under him. He spun backward and landed on his buttocks. This means war, he shouted, you punks are history. The boys feared that their amusement would only increase the punishment but they couldn't help laughing. Nothing was better than flattening T.O. Somehow in attempting to ram the front door down with a telephone pole the truant officer wedged himself underneath the foundation of the shack. He had no air. But before being smothered to death he tunneled his way out. Similar to the bow and plunger he had used earlier the boys retaliated with a blast from their equally homemade watermelon bazooka. The heavy watermelon, with its seeds, rind and sweet juice, splattered the truant officer's face, again knocking him onto his rear end. Once composure was regained the truant officer set the fort on fire. He told the brothers to come out with their hands up. They had assaulted a law enforcement officer. They were resisting arrest. If they wanted to play hardball then look out fella. There was no response. The shack continued to burn. The door popped opened. There was no one inside, only three lumps in the bed—no doubt the hiding boys. Amid a cloud of smoke the truant officer pulled the covers off to reveal what appeared to be three burnt little bodies folded up on their knees. They bore a distasteful resemblance to barbequed chickens. In a state of utter desperation the truant officer threw himself on the floor and wept. He had burned the children alive. He had turned them into little pieces of crispy meat. Bring them back, he cried. All I wanted to do was scare the hell out of them, jam their faces up against the furnace so they never disobeyed me again. Now it looks like murder, like I murdered three boys. They'll put me away for life. Please bring them back.

As I remove my eyeglasses from my pinched, lifeless face and rub them clean with my shirt sleeve, I point with a ruler at the chalkboard of goodwill. If the story I was telling had the feeling of a morality tale then we were all leaning in the same direction. It's no different than Donald Duck and his three nephews. I must embarrass myself and break wind behind the curtain of extensive knowledge and confess my kinship with those young boys. All I mean to say is that I would like to be the *fourth* brother. A boy outside of the story, but very much a part of the gang. Perhaps not by blood, not biologically, yet I wish to retain the blood, a thick, greasy mud, that I take for granted—held loosely under my skin, circulating in a manner unknown to me. I do take a certain pleasure in bleeding others, which is to say, I am very much with the three in spirit. The brothers will return in a visceral way and resume the fecal pleasures of story-telling, taking it down a dark hole of their choice. It is easier for them to become me than me them. I'd slow them down. I was invisible before I blundered in. It is best if I slither back out and return to that discreet place of caution and good judgment. But first let me say that we sit in terribly pint-sized chairs that cause us to bulge, like the bloated creatures we really are, and then when we feel small enough, shrunken, beaten down we find ourselves in gigantic overstuffed chairs in which our aching limbs cannot reach the armrests. These miserable chairs of loose upholstery threads, which we count on for support, fray and smell like our own miserable bodies. Nothing truly fits. That's what being alive is all about. Consciousness, the cruelest prison. The beautiful places we escape to are a flimsy backdrop compared to the grating pressure that hounds the small but oh-so-substantial inner brain. Everything is crammed into a hole until it is ripped up, sore and drippy. We cannot help but take pleasure from these tragic procedures. We crave a secret. The ebb and flow of caprice is a chewy paste. It sticks to the roof of our mouths, unwilling to dislodge a chunk of joy. Citizens honor the stars and stripes of real estate by cruising their malignant vehicles up and down Hollywood Boulevard, shouting, I am here, this is my spot. A squatter with an exhaust pipe. As teeth fall out of our gums we demand less government until we're represented by no one, least of all ourselves. Once removed from society we gleefully rape and pillage our neighbors' flowers; that's the pattern, splashing around in highly ordered anarchy. The few good men the marines are snooping around for are not the boys in this story, even if they sit in automobiles and pick their noses like the common taxpayer. The story I have stopped telling waits like a good little doggie. It begs to go out, wants another treat. If I wasn't on my way out I'd kick it to death just to break the sentimentalist's heart. In a court of law the Old Testament is under every palm, but the confident lies that boom out of every mouth are looked upon as the new truth. Remember, good men lie. Having said all that, it is now important to ask how a government employee, the truant officer, could do this (slay, slaughter, butcher...finish, mangle, rub out, do in) to three innocent young citizens. It's beyond comprehension. Burned alive. Decapitated and gutted, their hearts, livers and brains stuffed back into their chests through their enlarged anuses. To repeat these actions in words may, in some circles, be considered as reprehensible as the actual gruesome deed (blood in the mind no different than blood on the hands, the thought/sin equation) but in this circle, the circle of boys and brothers, of ditching school, hanging out and goofing around, where rectums and entrails are comical and fascinating, it must be done. Who would do such a thing? Mutilate and start giggling? I do whatever the other boys do.

So the truant officer called out to Jesus Christ. As flames jumped up all around him he rubbed his nose into the gravel floor and threw his massive, plumberlike rear end into the air. Oh, Jesus, please forgive me. I know not what I have done. I mean, I know what I've done, I just can't believe how stupid I am. Make this not be true. Put their heads back on. Tell them to cuss and spit at me. And at that moment an angel floated down on a string from the ceiling. It had wings and a halo. The angel spoke to the truant officer. It told him that because of the nature of the crime he'd have to stand in the snow and ring a Salvation Army bell for the rest of his life, that there was nothing Jesus could do. The Lord is not, nor has he ever been, in the business of turning back time. The angel's wings began to burn away and the ephemeral halo was also in jeopardy. Just then the truant officer heard giggles from the rafters and saw two of the brothers poised on a beam. The truant officer flew into another violent rage. Should he really be working with children? He grabbed the angel boy and chased the other two down and tied them all up and marched them chain-gang style all the way to school. A sign on the back gate read: SCHOOL CLOSED FOR SUMMER VACATION. They didn't have to be there. They could play all they wanted. He'd dragged them all that way for no reason.

With classes no longer in session the truant officer felt worthless, cut adrift from the rest of the world. He moaned like a sick cow. In a state of total anguish his eyes, mouth and cheeks contorted into a series of stretchy horror masks. His two arms, the long left one and regular (but short by contrast) right one, flapped uncontrollably like thick rubber cables in a wind tunnel. He tracked children down for a living. He could have hurt them. He *did* hurt them. Was he put on earth to kill children? He wondered. That's what some people do—bang them around like toys, chew them up like soft meatloaf. He didn't feel well. He started to walk down the street and then stopped. He turned left, walked some more, stopped again. He turned right and groaned. It was July and he thought it was Christmas. How come no reindeer? He couldn't figure out why he never saw giraffes wandering loose in the public parks, why there were no reports of lion maulings.

The boys, who'd been observing him, said, You said we could spit at you, kick you and cuss. Maybe you would even let us kill you. We could cut you up slowly, beat you with a tire iron, hang you upside down, wake you up with boiling or freezing water. We read about torture techniques in a book we stole from the survivalist store. Without proper funds a person must steal to survive. We know just where to bring down a hatchet onto the medulla, for example, or how to take an individual out through strangulation, via hand, wire or rubber hose. We know medical words that frighten our parents but impress our teachers. Just as *Moby Dick* was a nineteenth-century allegory about the bourgeoisie's war against the proletariat, so is this a diminutive tale of extremes.

The truant officer, our contemporary Ahab, the bossman who eternally exploits the worker, said, Do what you want, take me to your church.

The four of us pushed T.O. back to the fort. The wooden exterior had burned away, leaving only a steel and concrete bunker, a scenario we'd anticipated for months. Burn us alive and shout, I'm innocent, I only meant to return them to school. We know all about the strategies of tyrannical government employees. How they weed out the undesirables through accidents. We kicked T.O. to the floor and hoisted him up by the ankles with a rope and pulley. We are short (half his size); we used a ladder. The procedure was difficult but we were organized and determined. We stripped him naked. His fat stomach looked odd pointing in the opposite direction. We always called him a pig. We had no idea that he'd actually look like one, hanging upside down with no clothes on. T.O. began to cry. We told him to quit acting like a baby but he refused. We placed a bucket under his head and then pulled out a scalpel. We made a deep incision the length of his belly. A stream of blood dripped down. His intestines fell out like Christmas toys from a stuffed shopping bag. The purple sausages flopped in front of his face. They untangled all by themselves, creating an erratic eight-foot circle on the floor. T.O. vomited, completely missing the bucket. He was not angry but as we sewed him back up, leaving his intestines on the outside of his belly, he shouted in a disagreeable manner. We gave him a quart and a half of blood, a pint from each of us. The following day we lowered his body to a horizontal position and fed him four little potatoes. He appeared to enjoy them. He requested a cup of coffee. We countered with Coke. We brought him a chair. Seated, facing us, the naked truant officer, with his intestines dragging on the ground, was our own personal monster, tame and smelly, twitching like a repentant and rickety sin machine, a personality type we're just now coming to understand. He picked at his stitches until they were all gone. At the same time each day we heard a dog barking outside. We brought him a radio so he could listen to the Brewers game. We are somewhere in Wisconsin. He said he could picture everything like it was a boardgame. The players had peculiar names, like Yount and Molitor. We had never seen a person have sexual intercourse. We wanted T.O. to have sex. We brought in the barking dog. It was silent, approached cautiously. It licked T.O.'s toes and face and chewed up several feet of intestines. T.O. petted the dog's back. The dog scratched the ground involuntarily. The dog appeared anxious. He looked up with an intelligent but meek expression. T.O. reached into the dog's mouth and pulled out its tongue. The dog ran around in a circle, making a terrible sound, until we stopped it. T.O. hadn't learned anything. We peed on him, all of us at the same time. He enjoyed that. This is how we spent our summer vacation. On September 12 we stole a giant pair of blue jeans and a flannel shirt from Sears for T.O. and asked him to put them on. It was the first day of school and we wanted him to look warm and soft so the students would be attracted to him rather than repelled.

Mr. Eulogy

HE WAS LYING face down, still wearing his clothes, the head in a great pool of blood; on both lateral and posterior surfaces there were broad and deep incisions that penetrated the brain to a considerable depth in several directions; the head must have been struck many times, since the crown of the skull could easily be detached; a blow had also been struck to the nape of the neck without damaging the cervical vertebrae; several other blows had been struck to the shoulders and had cut through the sweatshirt and other clothing. These last-mentioned injuries, however, were not in themselves very serious; I did not consider any immediate action, since the brain and cerebellum were completely mangled; the arteries traversing them had been entirely severed.

FOR A WHILE no one I knew died. Obviously that was something to be thankful for, yet for some giant stupid reason I didn't take it that way. Living without tragedy, in a peaceful void, proved difficult, almost painful. People were crying all over the city but it happened too far away from my face for me, the center of the universe, the unblinking eyeball of all eyeballs, to feel anything. This lack of extremes, a veritable turnpike of emptiness, left me cracked and lardy. I had nothing of my own to mourn. A craving for trauma is typically associated with soldiers who return home from blood and dismemberment and can't face the approach of a mailman without going berserk (diving under the table, bellowing like a hound, leaping through windows, blasting a gun at their own face). As far as I'm concerned... it's my belief...I could...face practically anything. Here are a few examples of minor horrors endured.

When I was a child my mom used to scream at the top of her lungs to jar the hiccups out of my chest. That was her personal remedy and it rarely worked. I got hiccups every day because I was nervous and didn't breathe evenly through my nose. She'd hide behind a door and jump out at me. She'd make this horrible clicking sound as she tickled my scalp with one of her bony paws and say a spider was on my head, or she'd squeeze my arms, shake me and then say, All gone. My mom thought she could rattle away whatever ills crawled inside me and believed I enjoyed her treatments. My father paid no attention to these regular, one-sided assaults. A tooth was chipped after she struck the back of my head while I licked soda off the kitchen table. Once she tried to strangle me with the telephone cord. Her cooking was another brand of comforting punishment. As I threw up her many undercooked frozen dinners, she'd inform me that I was God's perfect child. She was a follower of the Christian Science church and therefore a big reader of Mary Baker Eddy. To her, barfing was a genuine religious experience. God was cleansing me. And she was correct. As I let loose a torrent of sour meats, she'd hover above me and say, There is no life, truth, intelligence or substance in matter. I'd think, there's a lot of substance in this matter; it might not be intelligent, but it sure is chunky. She'd say, Spirit is immortal truth, matter is mortal error. Spirit is the real and eternal, matter is the unreal and temporal. Spirit is God and you are his image and likeness, therefore you are not material, you are spiritual. She'd play with the top of my head and tell me to get it all out. I was God's barfing child.

Like any child I expected the worst, the obvious. Would my mom leave me at the grocery store? Sell me? Drive me off a cliff? Get in bed with me?

93

Tear out my eyes? Does the man sitting on the park bench really want to kill me? All these things were possible. If an emergency would occur, I planned to go under the house. That's where I stashed the family flashlight. My parents had a supply of canned goods in the garage, where I stored gold coins, pliers, pitch fork, switch blade, ice pick and whip. An enemy should expect to be stabbed in the heart and carved into oblivion. To my parents the world was threatening in more obvious ways: every insect poisonous, every dog rabid.

These scenes actively return to me with the smell of sulfur and speak as if they can't live without me, as if they were meant only as tender family jokes. My parents were monsters who had jobs, and when they talked to other people, those addressed nodded and appeared to understand them. When I'd have to talk to my parents they'd look at the ground and say, gore...rowrff... and walk off with their heads down. As I advanced into boyhood all conversation between us stopped. Even grunts ceased. Suddenly nothing mattered. All these people I went to school with, nothing was going to stop their cheerful, euphoric, idiotic progress. But I was sullen and stagnant. None of my friends was especially healthy (they never went to the doctor or dentist, and none of them had health insurance) but they all, independent of one another, managed to stay alive. As a bored yet respectful citizen of the world I stared out my window—and saw, of course, nothing. I watched the television (given to me by a fellow employee at a job I have long since quit—or was I fired? I'm no longer ashamed to admit it) and it showed me strangers oozing out of charred planes (or so I imagined); bagged bodies carried away on stretchers; remarkably distorted cars that had slammed into walls, telephone poles or other cars; guns that exploded in people's faces (that's what I heard, point blank range, but they never showed actual footage; again I was forced to imagine this). But everyone I knew (friends, relatives, neighbors) woke up every morning with nothing more than a headache or a sore throat, and of course it was always this minor ailment that was exaggerated in their minds and caused them to whimper as if someone had torn out their fingernails or perhaps peeled away a layer of their flexible, unfreckled epidermis. I have freckles. I was surprised to discover that the light brown spots are suspended within the layers of my skin. I always imagined myself to be spotted deep down to the core. Constantly sinking, unwilling to cry.

95

THE LAST TIME I saw him he was absolutely still, lying on his back, his feet resting against the fireplace, his right hand at his side, the fingers contracted, the left hand clenched on the breast, the clothes in fairly good order except for a coffee stain down the front of his shirt. As disorganized as things appeared, the room was curiously peaceful. I hummed a song. The shades were drawn. I was fascinated. A huge pool of blood encircled the head like a massive shadow; the right side and front part of the neck as well as the face were slashed to such a degree that the cervical vertebrae were wholly severed from the trunk; the head was still connected by skin and muscles on the left side; a bone on the right side was completely crushed; the blow extended toward the crown of the skull so deeply that the greater part of cerebral substance was separated from it (it's a wonder how so much material fits neatly into such a small container); several other blows had struck the face with such violence that bone and muscle were reduced to a pulp.

I HAVE FILES on all my friends. In Terry's I have a photo of his mother. I must've stolen it. I can't see why he'd have given it to me. But would I steal a photograph of someone's mother? Mothers were always like cops to us. They assumed we shoplifted, picked fights and received stolen property. Maybe it was during one of Terry's cleaning frenzies, when everything he saw went directly into the trash. In the picture his mom is younger than we are now, which is thirty. She's kind of awesome: sweet, cool, hip. She is also dead now, so she's a was, not an is, a part of history. She looks intelligent and beautiful. I must've liked that. I was proud that I knew Terry's mother when we were severe drug fools. I have an odd fondness for that time. It was our sloppy, inside version of a proper education. We were scholars of the encyclopedia of boredom and euphoria. She thought I was a good influence on Terry, that I might set him straight, keep him out of future trouble. That's because one day she asked him to clean something, he resisted and I talked him into it. She thought I was an angel after that. She thought, Sensible, trustworthy boy. I thought, she's the anti-mom, a mature awesome babe—let's rock. But I was scared every minute. Parents believe either that you're worse than their children, a destructive presence, or that you're a role model; but you're never moral equals. During college, with the occasional exception, we were grotesquely similar. We dressed and slanged our words like twin parrots, looked at the same magazines, burped and farted for each other's enjoyment, wolfed down thousands of pizzas. At the time I wondered what my friends' parents looked like naked. For some weird reason they all seemed hot, like over-the-hill porn stars. Mothers' cleavages squeezed out of floral blouses while fathers' leathery gonads poked out of bermuda

97

shorts. They were the only strangers who were generous and friendly to us. They'd buy us things, minus the clean-the-garage blackmail.

At Terry's memorial service everyone's stare vibed me onto another planet. The crowd was crushed with death-sorrow. Normally I would have exploded in an anarchy of hysterics, which would've disgusted the parents, but it was assumed I felt the worst, so I held on by biting my lower lip and surreptitiously yanking underarm hairs. He was my number-one bro. I was hugged twenty-three times. I wore sunglasses. More than sadness, I felt totally nervous because I was giving a speech. It was something I'd secretly lived for. To reveal intimate truths about a friend to the hordes. I knew the dead Terry better than anyone living. Once we were all inside church, the priest spoke. He pleased the family and pissed off the friends, Father Yellowbrains, saying something about Terry's spirit commingling in the fertilized garden of quietude. It was bogus and rank. He also quoted Rod McKuen. Then it was my turn. I climbed four steps to the altar, turned left and approached the pulpit. My shoes were old but they still made loud noises. I wore a grayish black T-shirt. It was boiling that day. I was more nervous than I'd ever been, but I thought I triumphed. I talked about what great friends Terry and I were, where we hung out, the sad and the funny stuff. People laughed in between or through their tears, which was a relief. I thought I was going to confess something ridiculous, like, say, I was a fraud, I didn't have any right to be alive, that I should be the one lying in the casket, wearing the blue suit. I said something about the time he called me his best friend and how much that floored me. I always thought Terry was too cool to use such a romantic expression. I didn't think people had best friends anymore. Terry was very tall. Everyone in the room knew how handsome he was. We treated him like a senator. We would've applauded when he entered a room if it wouldn't have pissed him off. He was strong, freckled, and Waspy. He smoked Lucky Strikes. Sometimes when he talked his mouth would pinch as if he had a pain in his stomach, as if he hated the ordinariness of his thoughts though they were never ordinary. He was an extreme and comical thinker. A woman in the back row, overwhelmed by the greatness of her loss, cried perfectly. She was blowing her nose. Crying is so intense. I envied her. She was immersed in sorrow. I needed to cry or else it wouldn't seem right. I started to imitate her, slowly, without looking like a fake. I was getting close, a tingle, and then a distinct quake. I knew I was going to cry, I could feel it in my thighs; they were heating up. My stomach tightened up and pushed out, my chest sank in. The grief was crawling up my body like mercury. It was as beautiful and scary as anything I had known. I said Terry drove like a maniac and screamed cool and lewd remarks at other drivers, and how he loved egg salad sandwiches and

99

when he ate them they'd ooze out of his mouth in a funny way. I was freaking. My throat was seized and my mouth stretched down into a wild frown. My eyes and forehead gathered up in a thick wrinkle. I must've looked pitiful, but that was good. Everything collided in the middle of my body. My vision blurred, my thoughts jumbled. I began to shake. Tears filled my eyes and then fell from the outermost corners of my eyelids. They were there for everyone to see; two long fat streams. I thought of wiping them away but I was too pleased and self-conscious to do it correctly. I tried to stay rigid. Me, the strong one, the leader of weepers, crying harder than anybody.

THIS IS A PURE Terry-thought. Could a person cry if he only had an eye socket, if one of his eyeballs had been removed? If not, wouldn't it be awkward to cry from the left eye while the right one was dry and untroubled?

WHEN I WAS AN insect human of thirteen years I beat up my friends and sat on them. When they cried I stuffed them under my bed with a blanket and pillow and told them to shut up or else my mom, the prison guard, would enter and scratch them to death. When she pushed the door open I'd already have the radio turned up, and if she asked what all the pounding was about if she'd say, That screaming, it sounded like two people. Was anyone crying? Are you hiding someone in here?—I'd say I was doing push-ups, practicing some wrestling moves. She believed everything I told her. When she left I'd extract my pal from under the bed and tell him my mom loved it when I hurt people: She's a female Satan and you should see what she does. I wasn't lying about this. She was sinister. She froze and boiled animals. Flesh was her friend. She hated the shocking color of blood, but she loved its high temperature as it left the body.

101

I WAS NEVER the one, the all-knowing god, the first to hear the news. I was always a micro-disciple, the last to know about everything: new albums, parties, who broke up with whom. Whenever I told someone that so-and-so died, they'd stare back at me as if a chunk of snot was swinging from my nose, then they'd say, God, dung-wad, we knooow. Everyone, always and forever, already knows every-thing.

Finding Terry's body was the backstage pass I needed. Before Terry, whenever a person I knew died I drew a blank. The blank bothered me, made me nervous, like I was in some way responsible. I'd twist up my numb insides and decide I was heartless. People'd watch me not react and, of course, dislike my behavior. Not having appropriate things to say about the death or the deceased or whoever was left alive was horrible. That's the cruel thing. The loss of a friend is supposed to bring out one's greatest feelings.

Friends die for friends and someone ends up being the hero. Sometimes the dead guy, sometimes you. It's the one big thing friends do for each other. I know I seem ungrateful but I'm not. I've never been more appreciative. I think about Terry dead and I think, what an act of generosity. It's a big sacrifice. I stand around and endure. When Terry died my first thought was, unfucking real, and then, thank you. I said, Thanks man, thanks for dying and shit. I'm going to make you into the coolest in everyone's head, don't worry, and thanks for turning me into a legend, too.

MARY WAS THE greatest person on two feet. That's how I began her eulogy. She had big feet, size eight. She walked with a heavy step though she wasn't fat, just big-boned. She was incredibly sexy. It was her religion to be strong and never complain. She could survive anywhere. She was the best pal a guy could expect out of a girl. She drank beer and whiskey. She could catch any football or baseball I threw at her. She tuned-up her own car and rotated the tires. She sewed up the upholstery when it cracked. Once she smashed a beer bottle over the head of a kung fu psycho who was trying to kill me. He threw her on her head. She was knocked out for a few seconds but it didn't bother her one bit. She was a hero all the time. She always had a big appetite. One of her favorite meals was cheese and crackers. She'd slice up a quarter block of cheddar and stack the slices on top of crackers and position them by her elbow while she read a book. When we first met I thought I was going to burst into flames. I used to call her Louie because she had long curly hair like the Sun King, Louis XIV of France. She didn't mind that name. For a Christmas card one year she cut out a picture of Louis and pasted it to a tin foil star and wrote, Merry Christmas from the Sun King. I thought that was the greatest thing in the world. I'm staring at it now.

103

She was lying on her back, wearing black pantyhose, her other garments disordered, her head bare except for a pink alligator hair clip. Clumps of her hair had been pulled out and were lying at her feet, her arms were crossed over her breasts; the bib and the kerchief had been torn away, which showed that she had put up some resistance to her murderer. At the right side of the neck one could observe a broad and deep incision that had severed not only the skin and muscles but also the carotid artery; the second cervical vertebra had been cut through completely. Above this first incision were several others running in the same direction but not so deep; they had been arrested by the ascending branch of the lower jaw; the face was scored in various directions with broad and deep wounds; the lower jaw was also severed near the symphysis of the chin; the upper jaw was severed by a blow that, having struck above the orbits, almost penetrated the brain; an oblique incision from right to left completely severed the nasal cavity.

I HAVE A PROBLEM with my right nostril. I've been picking it madly for weeks. It feels like a little ice pick is in there, jabbing at the inner lining. I think it's infected. I have a rotting nostril.

CHRISTMAS IS NEARING. It is December 9, my birthday. Worried about sleep. A stupid problem. Sleep is anti-life. It's losing the losing. Why can't I consume the extra time and live more? One hanging head, a guilty Fred. Since I haven't done anything worth losing sleep over I can go on not feeling terrible. I feel good. I wrote my parents a letter. I told them that I heard I was doing well. I said I was Santa Claus, the busy bloated pig. I wrote, Don't worry about that son of yours, he's having the time of his life. He's kind of a goblin but isn't scaring anyone. He stays in line all by himself, unlike me, who keeps eating and eating and farting and burping. Would you believe Santa doesn't have a single helper? No snowy elves or little cave bears to help him carry the heavy sack of presents. I am old and tired. All I eat is chocolate and black beans. The man in the moon has this grin that won't go away and it's scaring everybody on earth a lot. Being the single-minded parents that I know you are, your main interest in this letter is whether your son is happy or not. When I fly over his roof I look down and see a very cheerful character.

HE WAS SITTING in a chair. He was curled up in a ball. He was hanging from his feet. He was all over the place. He was fully dressed. His face was green, his head tilted back. His mouth was open. He was naked. His eyes were removed. His severed tongue rested in his left palm. The mattress was soaked. The sheets were shredded. The face was missing. Splattered blood covered all four walls. The skull was cracked, the brains spilled out. The head was sewn on backwards. The arms were shattered. Both ears were floating in a glass of bright red milk. The feet were bruised. The toes were burned. A yo-yo was in his mouth, a green olive in each nostril. A shovel, a baseball bat, a cleaver, a wire hanger, a broom, a plunger, a Ken doll, a light bulb, an apple, a carrot, lemons, salt, coffee grounds.

WE PAUSE IN OUR activities this afternoon to pay a richly deserved tribute to the memory of a devoted and highly esteemed individual. Dead Mr. Blank accomplished many difficult things during these trying times. He was a man of the greatest talents, a man of unparalleled humanity. He had a distinguished record in his particular field. He was one of the great whatevers of our time. Under his skillful and arduous influence his colleagues and fans were able to enjoy his remarkable projects. No matter how difficult the endeavor he had a brain bright enough to grasp the most complicated idea and reduce it to its simplest elements. He was truly one of the great ones. Men sought his advice because they knew not only of his integrity but of the care and impartiality by which he arrived at the conclusions that helped govern his mind. He was a man who made friends without making enemies. He was a man you didn't have to know for a long time in order to get the feeling that you knew him all your life. And now he is gone! You and I could not suffer a more sorrowful blow. He had a genius for finding out how he could be kind. He was bold in his kindness. His heart looked upon those that needed help as if they were brothers. He possessed a genius for friendship. His love of all people was manifested time and again by his devotion to all worthy causes, regardless of race, creed or color. We who knew him knew the greatness of his sorrow. Now that he is taken above to his Maker, we salute his memory. He was impressive, unselfish, moral, famous, courageous, warm, virtuous, noble, loving, patriotic. His sterling qualities live on. We express our great grief. Good-bye, faithful friend.

I CRUSHED LITTLE birds with stones and burned them. I chased dogs into the street until cars ran them over. I did all this. I know you'll think I'm lying—after all, I'm the greatest person in the world. My name is the same as other boys'. Even so, there is no one else but me. Every day I think the same thing. Every hour it's true. Other people only think they are that great, elevated person, while I truly am the one.

Sleepy all the time. Can barely get out of bed. Dirty sheets. Wouldn't dream of going to the laundromat right now. I'd rather die. Slept thirteen hours last night, ate breakfast, two-hour nap, layed around another hour. Watched part of a movie, a western, then a game show, then a talk show, all with the sound off. Farted sixteen times. Sounded like a dog, a trumpet, a kazoo, a duck, tearing fabric, all the thoughts in my head, a moist sneaker. Stared at the ceiling till nighttime. First it was six o'clock, then suddenly eleven. It's winter. Thought of going for a walk. Too tired, too scared, so I just stood there. I was in the bathroom and the kitchen, mostly. That was plenty tortuous, exhausting. Boring. Horrible breath. Pouring rain. Back inside. Much better, thinking about rain, hearing it bang on the roof like it wants to come in, and pretty soon it does, little by little, all the great leaks in my grungy chateau. I've been dreaming about this large person, a giant guy, trying to get me. I have a pistol but I'm too chicken to fire it. I hold it and feel stupid and weak. No matter how pathetic I become, it amazes me how there's always room to get worse. New wild lows. I think I'm still alive and that seems hilarious.

Artist and Fly

A FLY SWIRLS AROUND the center of the studio, avoiding all the windows and walls. This strikes him as odd—a fly not drawn to direct light, fresh air or a surface. Then again, what does he know about flies and the milieu they prefer?

Nothing. I'm not an expert. I never studied flies in school. I studied English but now I'm a painter. That's what this brush is doing in my hand. Black black black.

The fly cuts out for itself an invisible area with distinct borders—peculiar and ungainly figure eights. It's not traveling from room to room, investigating dust levels, gauging temperatures, or frantically searching for food. This fly is modest in its course. It's simply buzzing about on its unknown business, in the audience of a distracted man who paints eight hours a day (he times himself, subtracts lunch, phone calls and errands).

Lately he has a great deal of trouble making art. In terms of actual production he's slowed down to a crawl.

Lately I've been cranking this shit out.

He's tall and handsome. It's worked to his advantage.

I'm an ugly fuck.

Flies tend to make themselves known during the spring and summer, right? He thinks so. Never on a cold or rainy day. It's like they're all sleeping. This man hasn't chased a fly down in what feels like years. I'll just stand here and let it come to me. That's how you do it. He takes a swing and a curve of black spatters the floor and wall. Missed. Now the fly's over there.

What about those loud flies? Why so loud? This one's silent. Are they just more physical than the quiet ones? Is it gender? I'm familiar with the kind of fly that spends its time by the window. What he means is, they're easier to kill. You don't knock stuff over, break things. A dead fly blends into the mesh of a screen—a webbed graveyard, if you will. My world view. Quote me.

He drops the paint brush on a sheet of wax paper and rolls up the first magazine he sees into a weapon. *ArtForum*. No, can't use that one—his last show was reviewed in there (a pan, a good pan; he thinks it's hilarious but he'd still like to see the reviewer dead)—nor the one under it (there's an ad for the show on the inside back cover). How about this older one? He's not mentioned in it at all. Nor has he read it yet. Nor will I ever. You see, if there are fly guts on it he'll throw it out. Even if he washes it off it'll sicken him. But that's the feeling I get whenever I crack open that rag. Everyone knows what those pages are really for. Same as the leaves in the woods. A dead fly. Two days dead. Then three, four, five and counting. The tiniest reminder of violence will set him back for hours. Makes me nauseous—which is strange, considering how violent my imagination is. What's his name, the British wad, said my paintings are about fear. I guess he's not totally off. It's the Lacan, Roland Barthes footnote bullshit that makes me want to let loose a brown bomber.

Each day at 3 P.M. he takes a long nap. He usually dreams of strangely normal things. This week it's people with large white teeth. Why teeth? he thinks. Mine aren't so bad. A little crooked, not too yellow. What do I care about good teeth? This is troubling to him. Am I worried about being eaten? By whom? He can see his emotions splashing out of a bathtub, and gets further upset at the thought of the bathwater soaking through the linoleum (has this been happening for years?), rotting the foundation. That's what vermin thrive on. Moisture. And I just made a down payment on this space, God damn it.

He grabs a newspaper and rolls it up. He tightens it so it's hard and manageable. The fly demonstrates it quickness, continuing on its random esoteric course. He swings at the fly, buffoonishly slow. The noise of a fly, that thick heavy buzz, is terribly irritating (it's not a quiet fly after all). Work, serious or otherwise, especially painting, can't be done with such a distraction. He has gone from a rational human being, this example of a man (don't get objective with me), to something unsightly, an absurd, wasteful character. That's fine. I never intended to be memorable.

He recalls other flies that've flown through the studio. Oh, yes, I called one the sleepy fly. This fly behaved like it grew up in an icebox. A groggy frozen fly that couldn't get airborne. It was a zombie, the undead of the fly world, and depended on the kindness of a few strangers (man, spider, cat) to refrain from killing it. This sleepy fly, goofy in its drunkenness, pathetic and supremely vulnerable, landed on my arm and waited to be petted. I brushed it onto the table. Maybe it's just not feeling well, I thought; or has it eaten something terrible? No, no, its favorite food is shit, what am I thinking? Or was it depressed, very old, in its twilight years? Yes, that's a little more like it. The end of life. The sleepy fly staggered onto the lip of a cup. It trembled; its eyelash legs couldn't hold up that big body. I smashed that fly so hard I broke the cup, a sacrifice. I turned it into speckled mush. Purely dead. I held it up to other living flies as a warning. Look, this will happen to you.

Experienced boxers have no trouble catching flies. That's how he starts talking to this fly, as if the fly were his opponent in the ring. Out loud he tells the fly he's going to fuck him over. That he's going to beat his ass. You're going to wish you were never born. Then he imagines a promotional poster of the little fly, maybe double its actual size, which is still no bigger than his own wide thumb nail, and himself, looking disgruntled, disoriented and sweaty, clad in satin boxer trunks, holding a rolled-up newspaper. The two, scheduled to meet on Christmas Day at Caesar's Palace.

How I Made Certain of My Art

THE NAKED HUMAN body is real beauty. Have you ever drawn a picture of a naked human body, a nude person, man or woman? My wife, she's dead now, she was an artist and the last painting she did was of a tiger in a very grassy meadow with tropical birds, palm trees and a blue stream—and do you know what was on the tiger's back? Would you believe, a nude woman? Lounging on the violent beast as if it were a skinned version of itself on some rich man's floor by the fireplace.

I'm a professional photographer in my spare time: *Newsweek*, *Omni*, *Playboy*. She knew she was dying, God bless her, and she asked me to do a mammoth photographic reproduction of her masterpiece. And I did. It was my memorial to her.

I bought the most expensive lenses in the world and the most expensive filters and I went to the zoo and took detailed close-up photographs of the tiger. I chose the meanest looking eight-hundred-pound tiger of the bunch. I could tell he must've ripped open many an elephant, bear, buffalo, crocodile, deer, cow, wild hog. I took seventy-two photographs of just the tiger's eye alone—I captured the tips of a palm leaf embedded in reflection across his yellow eyes—and so many more photographs of the white whisker hair in the cheeks and chin. I grew to respect the raw intelligence of the animal. When I looked through the camera's viewfinder and stared deep into the tiger's eyes I felt a sudden masculine affinity. He was me: I was him. I was the tiger in my wife's mind's eye. I photographed hundreds of blades of grass and then I photographed my wife naked, all of her hair and all of her skin. Then I cut all the photographs into tiny squares and glued them to the biggest wall in my house.

That's about the time she passed away. Things grew dark but I kept the lights on. I lined up the pictures of her blue eyes on our bed, rows and rows of them, a field of poppies. She looked rested. I missed her. I swear, her nudity, that natural state, is pure art. On the floor I pressed my mouth against sections of her thigh or chest and kissed them. The sensation of the satin finish moved me. 4" x 5". Borderless.

I would rush home from work, boil some franks, and then start gluing. A clear mind was essential, so the liquor was off limits; but then my thinking began to sag, so the gin and tonic were allowed back. I practically went blind, sweated, took ice cream breaks, didn't show anybody, told some guys at work, next thing I know this art collector guy calls me on the phone, says he heard from another art collector that I was the guy who made one giant photograph from thousands and thousands of small photographs, and could he see.

Fellow comes over and two seconds later writes me out a check for five hundred thousand dollars. Imagine that.

I pulled out some fresh bologna and mayo, put them between bread, trimmed the crust, sliced them four ways, abracadabra: cocktail sandwiches. He ate them all. Don't think the rich aren't hungry. Newspaper crew came and took a photograph of it, one photograph of all those photographs. It was in the paper the next day. I was in the photograph, too, smiling beside the tiger, the subconscious me, and my wife and a caption: WIDOWER MEMORIALIZES NAKED WIFE.

Day later, the art collector came by with his crew but they couldn't peel the pictures off the wall. So they took it, took my wall. I didn't mind—hell, one large room instead of two small ones. More space to prowl in. He told me that I could come over to his home in Albuquerque and visit my dead naked wife, anytime.

I donated all the money to a children's hospital. I love children.

House Monument

Battle

I TALK LITTLE KIDS in the neighborhood into whomping on each other. After school I set them up in my parents' backyard. I make up terrible stories about their mothers and fathers and I whisper these things to them and accuse each of the other boys of having told it to me. I do that for a while and then I say that it's wrestling time. I sound the bell. I say *ding* and start pushing one kid into another. I grab one kid's fist and strike it against the other's head. Then I grab the other kid's head and say, Ouch, I'm not going to let anyone hit me, especially someone who says your mom is an ugly hag. Then I grab his fist and slug the other kid. I take a step back and tell them to defend their parents and kill. Danny is the smartest kid. He can sense what I'm doing. He looks at me perplexed, knowing what I've organized. But then he turns red and charges like a bull and the fun is underway. Punching, hair pulling, kicking, swearing. When one kid is losing I lie down next to him as he's getting lightly beaten up and inspire him with more insults like, he thinks your dad's a weakling. That usually fires up the boy to throw the other off his chest and regain the advantage. I continue whispering things in everyone's ear, to keep one blaze going or to start up a new fight with the other kids watching. Things start to peter out when they realize they're fighting their closest friends and it's all for my pleasure. The game usually ends once everyone's crying. I tell them they all fought well and I'll see them tomorrow for more. I say if anyone tells their parents they'll be sorry, and I laugh like a man of evil.

Splat

WITH GUYS MY own age we hang out at night, and if there's no big money to buy eggs we buy one pack of balloons and steal twenty more. We fill the balloons up with water. They're tricky to throw because they giggle in your palm; it's hard to get a good grip. But there's nothing better than eggs. The destruction quality is so high. We climb the hill on Valley Vista, where the big curve is, and bomb cars.

It takes practice to hit a moving car, even if gramps is at the wheel. We have our escape route all worked out so there's nothing anyone can do. People have tried. Here's an example. I nail a Corvette. The guy stops the car in the middle of the street, gets out and starts cussing. Says he's going to kill us. We know how tricky it is to climb that hill. You got to be a rodent. We laugh and taunt him to come up. We call him names. Geek, dork, fuckhead, slime, douchebag. Now the guy's really fuming, which cranks up the thrill another notch. He's climbing, digging his way up, losing his footing. We bomb him for a while. We know if he gets hold of any of us we're dead, and that's what's important. That's how we know how much fun we're really having. First we take off in the same direction. We go up to the top and hop the fence. This is where we all start to panic, and scatter. One time I watched Dave run full speed into a clothesline. It caught him right in the throat. I thought his head was going to come off. Nothing happened though. I was laughing my brains out and I asked him if he was alright and he said yes; he got up and we kept running. It was great. We know just where to go. The jerk is wasting his time. Over a couple more fences and suddenly we're miles away.

119

Six months later we're walking down Valley Vista and the same man in the Corvette remembers who we are and jumps out of his car and sprints toward us. I come close to winning the 50- and 100-yard dash in school so there's no way this fat businessman in wingtips is going to catch me. I could fake him out even if he was standing right next to me. If he ever got close enough to punch, I know how to dodge fists. I also know how to dodge cars if that's his plan. Plus, I have secret self-defense tactics. Pressure points, the temples, behind the earlobes, those'll kill you; or just one power uppercut straight at the nose so that the bone goes right through to the brain and the guy dies instantly. Everyone knows that.

House Monument

FAT CREEP BUYS another lot. He plans to build a house on it. Let him try. This block is for dirt bikes. Fat Creep is a realtor—in other words, a slobbering blubber God. Fuck him. I buried my riches in this soil: prehistoric tools and weapons, a ring of ancient keys; I buried bugs, lizards, birds, fish and some pretty big animals. Once I buried a deer. It came down from the mountain, ran up to me and died. Those things're skinny but they weigh a ton. And they're spooky-looking up close. They're not cute like most people think.

Fat Creep sees me standing at the edge of his lot and asks what I'm doing, if I'd like some help. Sure delux blob, point me north so I can get away from the stench of your flesh. I don't say that, though I would if I wanted to. If it was appropriate. I'd say, Drink this tinkle, moneybags, if I was in the mood.

The realtor's wallet bulges a few inches out from his butt like a weird growth. He looks like a hunchbutt. When I answer him and say, No, I don't need any help, he tells me to please find another piece of earth to speculate on. The audience laughs, the potential buyers, a nervous husband and wife team. Good use of the word speculate. I'm not speculating, I tell him; I'm mourning the death of my family. They were all killed last night. I fake-wipe a tear from my eye. An escaped convict broke into the house and hacked them all up. A terrible tragedy. I'm shaken. The police said they've never seen anything bloodier. The buyers frown. They give each other a look: Oh, dear, maybe this isn't the right place for us. The realtor knows I'm bullshitting. He erases me with a chuckle. He says, Our neighborhood storyteller. He shakes his head and waves me off like we were pals. He hates my guts. That's okay, I hate him more. He'd kill me if he had the chance. And would I kill him? you ask. No. That would make me nervous.

121

I walk across the street and sit on the curb. Fat Creep is being polite to me. If the buyers weren't beside him he'd waddle after me and yell something about the police, how they're going to drag me downtown and stick me in juvenile hall, or as my pals call it, juvie.

The buyers stand next to the realtor. They look like they haven't let go of each other's hands since they met, and what a beautiful day that must've been. I got nothing against them. What are people anyway? Mostly water. Just like the earth. I just have a little trouble with love right now. My girlfriend left me for this guy; he's sort of my friend, this hockey player. I was about to take her to get an abortion but my car wouldn't start. I tried to get a jump. In the meantime Karen freaks and calls my friend and he says hang on he'll be right over. He drives her to the hospital and they fall in love on the way there or on the way back. I guess he became her hero. My life has had a lot of ups and downs. Most of the time I feel like I'm going to explode, *blam*, like a cherry bomb, but then I just splash and roll around in my sleep like an oily porpoise and suddenly Fat Creep is building a new house and I'm in business.

He tells them that they are in a unique situation because he's also the supervising contractor. He'll see their baby through to the end. He always does. I can't say I stop him completely, but I get in the way. Even if he finishes, it takes him a lot longer than usual because I damage whatever he builds.

Once Fat Creep starts to build, here's what I do. At midnight, or one, or two, or once my parents are asleep, I drive my mom's station wagon over to the lot and stand around. The lumber smells okay. Some people go crazy for it like it's some kind of primal scent. They close their eyes and act earthy; they suck in the aroma and shake their heads to look for something that isn't there, then they rub their hands along the grain and say something about wishing they worked with their hands. But that thought ends with the next splinter. Most builders set the bathtubs in concrete right after they pour in the foundation. Those're my offices. I lie down in the tubs. I stretch out and stare at the sky. I wait for a shooting star. Living in the city, that can take hours. During those moments I feel kind of safe and not too unhappy. I think about what people said to me through the day, what terrible words I can save. Karen and I fucked in half of the tubs in this neighborhood. Giant sunken tubs are the worst. They're too big. It's like lying down in the middle of a deserted runway and both sides of the curb are out of reach. It still felt good. I don't want to think about that. Anyway, I heave as much lumber as I feel is necessary, which is usually all of it, into the station wagon, drive it home and store it in the backyard. Two-by-fours and sheets of plywood. I'm the family gardener, so my parents never know what's going on. At first I hated the job. Nothing worse than watering lawns and picking weeds. But then I built a toolshed—that's where I store my mer- chandise—and I told my father what kind of tools I'd need to make the grounds look nice. We went to the hardware store and he bought me an arsenal of weapons. Clipping shears, hoe, saw, shovel, pitchfork, and, of course, my two favorites: a sledgehammer and chainsaw. With a black marker I write something on the lumber, like my initials, or I just draw an X or a

123

swastika, so there's no doubt who the stuff belongs to. If my parents ask me about it I just say it's mine and walk away. They never have trouble with that. The quicker I end a discussion the easier it is to keep it meaning what I want.

I sell the lumber to people at school at low, low prices. Ken Norby buys the plywood to make these kick-ass surf paintings and Howard buys the two-by-fours for his fence business. They make perfect posts.

This repeats itself for a while, until they get the lumber installed—each room, four walls of wood. Next day they bring in the Sheetrock. I haul that away every night and just dump it in the L.A. River. No one I know needs any. Once the Sheetrock is installed I go in with my sledgehammer and bash head-size holes. Sometimes I go berserk and weaken the entire foundation with a few homerun swings. The gouges I make in the Sheetrock cause Fat Creep the most problems. The builders have to reorder new Sheetrock, pull off the old stuff and put it up again.

The next step is a visit from the realtor. He knocks on our door and reintroduces himself, usually to my mom (she works shorter hours and gets home first).

We've been over this before, he tells her.

I find this hard to believe, she says. This is ludicrous. Are you certain it's my son? He has a high regard for landscape. He's studying it in school. Look how he's taken care of our place.

You have a lovely house, Mrs. Martin. But I know the boy; I see him in the daylight. He loiters on my property. He disturbs my clients. For some reason he's picked me. I've even seen him carrying a hammer... (I'm in the bathroom listening, taking a fake shit) ...and I'm not going to stand for it. The next incident I call the police.

I don't think that'll be necessary, Mr. Owen. Why don't we have a talk with my son? I'm sure we can work it out. She yells my name. Great.

Hi, Mom. I'm right here, in the bathroom. I have diarrhea.

We don't have to know that, Ed, she says.

Shit is usually a showstopper. It worked again. 125

The police are so stupid they can't do anything. They'll just tell me to watch it. They'll give me the readymade look to try and scare me. All that does is make me want to cause more trouble.

Expressionism

WE ONLY KILL. They don't care if we do. Well, they do in a way. The prison gets a spotty reputation, the governor writes the warden a bossy letter and in the end most of our privileges are taken away, which means my painting time is threatened. I'm standing in front of an easel in the arts and crafts room, finger-painting a picture of a tree. The instructor doesn't permit brushes because we'll stab each other or ourselves. We will use them incorrectly. They care about us in a very particular way. Out the window, in the exercise yard, I see another fight. An ideal setting for a brawl. My fellow inmates are ripping each other to shreds. The battle appears random, though it involves, like always, two distinct gangs. Everyone seems to be having a good time. *Tie a Yellow Ribbon* is jingling away on the phonograph. One head is crushed with a barbell in hand, another neck hacked with a cleaver smuggled out of the kitchen. Now I know what some of us will be eating for dinner tonight. To die here is always the result of someone's pleasure. We have all these handmade weapons. Everyone stays up late, grunting, moaning, whispering, passionately sharpening the tips of their secret broom handles. To stop the fight below, the guards fire shotgun rounds into the air and at various feet. Some stop while others go at it harder, inspired by blasts. My tree painting is progressing nicely. All the different greens are so comforting. I didn't speak to anyone the first couple of years I was here. It no longer seemed necessary. Being here drained the meaning out of everything I could think of. Then it reversed. I became self-righteous and felt everything I thought was pure wisdom, coming straight from Jesus. Now my nest is somewhere in the middle. Jesus is very popular here, especially with the weightlifters. Many a dynamic crucifix can be seen sandwiched between damp and puffy pecs. Religion fits nicely into this way of life. The guy next to me, a resourceful fellow, is painting with his fist, rotating his arm in short, circular motions. He's not using any paint. He's speaking to himself. He's perspiring and of course saying something about his mother. He's grinding a hole into the center of the canvas. A sickly, acrid smell; something

127

burning, or so it seems. The skin has worn off his knuckles. The easel is rocking. The rim of the hole is turning pink. His knuckles are a bloody mess. He stops, stops painting, turns to me, smiles and says, Done.

The Why-I-Love-Violence Speech

Desert

THE CLOUDS NEVER formed one picture for very long. One minute it was a bearded man frowning, the next minute a pair of shattered teacups, the third minute three workboots descending in size. Yes, each minute a new surprise.

The only weapons available were rocks. They were all over the place. It was Land of the Happy Weapon so I grabbed a smallish one, nice and round with a tiny divot for my index finger to get a grip, and smashed it in your face. You went down like a drunken doll, all liquid and floppy. I thought, funny. One whack, blood running into the dried-up earth. Messy, but I don't have to clean up.

The cracks in the earth took you in like a drain, whether the dirt likes it or not; it doesn't know the difference between a decent creature and the world's worst.

SO YOU'RE STILL around in some way. Your friends might forget you but this sensitive hellhole remembers.

The earth bears witness to what I've done, absorbs the entire matter. Your bald head looks at home with all this rock. Boulder to boulder.

One little tap with a rock and that's it, you're out. I knew it wouldn't take much even though you always acted like Mr. Swaying Iron Gonads, but now there's not a whole lot happening in dem balls. No more arms akimbo, chest inflato; no more I'm-here-to-tell-you-what-to-do trash. I flipped you over, waited to see if you'd move, but you just laid there with your nose that made a sharp left on your face, your fucked-up lips open, like a big baby wanting another spoonful of banana mush. I kicked you in the stomach and your mouth closed. I kicked you a bunch more, moving higher and higher till I reached your face again. Then I jumped in the air and stomped down. I wanted to crush your skull, deflate that balloon brain of yours. I assume that's where your ability to count and remember names is stored. Somewhere behind the ears. Your flat oversized forehead always gave people the wrong impression. If I had a truck—and I still want one, a big square orange thing—I'd park it on your head and then roll it over different sections of your body until you were level with the road, so flat that your jawbone and cranium reformed into some shitty little pancake. The teeth would dislodge from your gums and bite into earth all cockeyed like a buck-toothed fool. I've wanted to kill you for so long it's hard to believe, and now that you're dead the fun's sort of over. But I can manage. I keep seeing all those stupid looks on your face through the years. That smile of yours is what moved me. Those gooey stones you have for eyes.

I'm going to leave you here. They call it desert meat. A big old uncooked sausage measuring six foot five, seasoned naturally on the exterior from its own juices and salts. Served raw at room temperature, on a bed of rock, we're proud to call him Horace Tartare. A bird or coyote will find you and be most grateful. That's got to be more than you ever hoped to achieve. I thought I could erase you but I was wrong. Soon you'll be part of the great American history of skeletons in the desert. The bony haunted things.

I'm thinking, time for a beer, just as every cloud in the sky leaves me with nothing to think about but an infinity of the darkest, most relentless blue.

Mountain

A SINGLE SHOT rang out through the trees but that's not going to disturb the pretty picture. Postcards of this landscape don't exist. Somebody's always humming but no one knows who. Brown sullen tree bark don't give a shit; it's glued to the fat pine.

My daddy put a bullet in her boyfriend's brain, or more precisely, blasted a shot right through the whole head, rendering the handsome buck faceless, permanently unable to come to the phone. No open casket for that spunky camper. His face looked like it was strip-mined. The woman grabbed her face and yelled *what* and then started running. Should we've repeated ourselves? We hadn't said anything, just stepped on some loud crunchy leaves, and then BLAMO. The shotgun sound sent an echo off the pine needles of every tree up and down the mountain, like it was a secret they had to bellow out in big hollow death language. This happy little mountain, filled with wolves and bears, sneaks into people's imagination and frightens them. There's no place to lie on your back and watch the sunset. It wasn't hunting season, yet. Elk knew that. As spooky as they are the trees never seem to mind what we do. They accommodate all sorts of activity, always able to see both sides of the matter, just like the old stumps in Washington, the Supreme Court judges; so by law, if

I, the scribe of this team, am reading the signs of life in the forest correctly, she was ours to keep, the woman. We found her. And now we find ourselves chasing her up the hill; she wasn't going to take this lying down, at least not in the beginning. Daddy said she'd make a perfect wife. We'd catch her and find out. She was built like a deer: strong thin legs, a firm soft-looking chest, giant brown eyes, and she was real quick. Her features connected like a curvy map I had already memorized. She was kicking up a dust trail, tripping over cones, so we were never going to lose her; plus we could hear her panting *oh oh oh oh*, like she was in pain, but we hadn't touched her yet and were never planning on hurting her. Even if your first thought is, kill it, eat it, hang the head on the wall, with her it's different; you think, she's a woman, remember; they're like people; you've got to love her like a mother or a saint or like your favorite dog. Pet her, let her lick you. But she's the one who'll prepare the food and shove it in front of you; she'll feed me, so technically I'm the dog, seated by his bowl. Maybe we'll each have a plate of food and eat together at the same time, then we'll strip and do the dog like married people, but daddy demands a front-row seat. Plus he's got first dibs on the woman. He says he's got to try her out for me—he's the expert, which is true— see if she's okay for his boy. That's always been the way we done it. We play the father and son routine like something fierce. I'm an expert at gutting fish. I

133

can hack a salmon's head and tail off and have her ready for the frying pan in under thirty seconds. We fish where the water smells like peanuts. We've been watching this girl for two days, saw them roll in and set up camp. Daddy said he's going to make love to her on the table. We've got a picnic table in the house. Isn't that crazy? Stole it from the campsite. Daddy says he likes fucking on the table so he can see it all clearly and he can walk away when he's done. He says a woman's belly is like a sacred meadow, all soft, and if they're muscular in the stomach they've got a quiet little ravine in the middle, speckled with a little fur. That's where he likes to unload his spray, so it puddles in the center. A microscopic fisherman could catch a shitload of some weird-ass tadpoles in that milky pond.

Irrigation Ditch

WHEN THE CIRCUS comes to town you have to be prepared for fun. So many good things happen under the big top. The sad clowns come out and play. They're so silly. Even though I flunked clown college I'm still a clown. I can't even eat a sandwich without spilling jelly down my front. But when the show's over the clown leaves his red nose on and gets fucked up on booze. Then he goes loony. He plays again, all by his little lonesome. But this time none of the children laugh and the stupid fat parents aren't bored anymore, especially after I, or after he, pulls the trigger of the squirt gun and wow, drills metal into your sweetbreads. Is that a warm thought, I mean, feeling? Don't you feel giddy? I know I do. Then the off-duty clown cuts you down to size with the goofiest hatchet and boils your bones—maybe I'm a witch, maybe I'm amazed—for a rude smelly soup, and throws away the parts he doesn't like into an irrigation ditch. Can't run very fast, oops, not with these big floppy shoes.

People among us live to cut off heads. I fuck to cut them up and shit Hail Mary. I cum all over myself in the hope that your head rolls down the street. I spray a load in the dirt. The fertilizer of tomorrow. Jackoff techniques have gone downhill. Accuracy and distance are an embarrassment. Clown fuck badly. Roll around in the mud with the sprinklers clicking over my head. Clown fuck funny: aims for eyes, only dribbles on cheeks. Clown fuck sadly, cum like tear drops.

135

Lunch

MY FAMILY TOTALS FOUR. Hardly an army. We walked into a restaurant and sat down. My mom looked across the room at the only other patrons, another family, all blonds. I was sixteen years old at the time. Within a minute she announced that the other family was a pack of Nazis. She said they were staring at us, all four of them; they were talking, and they weren't going to leave us alone. That much was certain. She demanded that my father do something. This is a true story. I'm not making up a word of it. My father said, what do you expect me to do, just go over there and start punching the guy? How can you be sure they're Nazis? I looked in the direction of the suspected family. They were motionless, not eating. They spoke a word or two to each other and looked directly at us. They were astonishingly blond. Large and celestial, yet oddly nondescript, glowing with Aryan wattage. I gave them my special death glare. They struck a cruel, slightly amused pose. I worried, if a battle erupted our weapons would have to be forks, spoons, napkins and butter knives. There were glasses filled with ice water, chairs, a table cloth. The waiters would most likely take the side of the Nazis. They were seated first and looked like fashion models. The mass appeal of blonds. They have more fun; they also kill more people. I knew my sister and mom could be trusted. I've fought them both. They are resourceful fighters. My mom once strangled me with a telephone cord and my sister punched a policeman who was trying to arrest a drug dealer. It wasn't her boyfriend—she just butted in, wanted a piece of the action. My father is a large thick man and I have the ability to be cunning and ruthless, I thought, or hoped, and I would not stop killing until the subject is as dead as a pulverized granule, which is to say, I believed we could take them in a fight. The man was younger than my dad but I was bigger than their son. I could finish him off in seconds. The girl wore a dirndl skirt and might've been hiding a rolling pin. Two thick braids hung stiffly from her head. I'd gouge their eyes out and bite their flesh. I'd stomp on their eyeballs the minute I saw them skitter across the floor. My mom was probably right about them being Nazis, but they were not wearing uniforms per se, or armbands. And if you removed my mom's paranoia we'd probably never have noticed them. Their curiosity or disapproval was just like anyone else's. The waiter asked us if we were ready to order. There was silence. My father said, Not yet. My mom said, Those people have a problem. What is their problem? Can you help us? The waiter said, I'll give you a few more minutes, and walked away. All at once, the other family stood up and marched out of the restaurant. My mom glared as harshly as possible like she was willing them away with her fierce hazel eyes, and I believe that's how it worked. As loving as she is the mommy tiger also has a frightful face.

Free-Thinking Christian Woman Writes

YOU ARE A WOMAN of the church. You live alone because you are single, not a widow. Based on this simple picture one can only believe, and rightly so, that you are a lesbian. Let's back up a step to the so-called olden days, two hundred years ago; if your hair was red or pitch black, and uncombed, and if you were in the habit of talking to yourself, men would see to it that a noose was slung over your head and that you dangled to your death from the limb of a tree. Or if the weather was right, a group of nervous men, assertive in packs, would burn you alive. Seeing an evil woman scream and fry up in orange flames convinces people that the path of homosexuality is the wrong route. Today's witch or lesbian is not so obvious. She takes good care of herself and is often indistinguishable from a heterosexual woman; therefore her punishments are far more discreet. I have seen pornography for lesbians and all I can say is...that metal and plastic equipment they jam up each other cannot be pleasurable—it simply does not belong inside a woman. Rub till the cows come home if the desire overtakes you. Continue rubbing, flicking and slapping (whatever the technique) at your crotch until these stubborn cows step into the bathtub and electrocute themselves. Throw the plastic, metal and rubber devices away. Erase all suspicion. Find a man, love him like a brother and marry him. If you're unable to change, don't kill yourself. There are men out there who are exactly like women, or men who are exactly like men but have the minds of women. They admit this. There are petite hairless men who smell like gardenias. There are tall and skinny men and round and jolly (or non-jolly) men. Sure most of them cum fast, but at least you have real flesh between your legs, and most of them apologize. There are men so quiet that if it's privacy you want, they will leave you alone for fifty years. What we're out to prove is that in some fundamental way, we're all the same; and *that* in itself is beautiful. If you don't change, if you remain a lesbian, you know what's in store for you. The day will come when you, along with many other perverse unfortunates, will be relegated to Earth As Ominous Oven, turned to broil, as we, the polished and unswerving Christians, take the celestial elevator to the Penthouse.

Today's happily married woman of the church—let's say things have progressed for her—is no longer the dowdy type who waddles down the sidewalk in her muumuu, with her four lovely children. She is still a strong mother with the same four vibrant offspring, as well as an enforcer of values, a strict disciplinarian, a devout and careful reader of the Bible... but she is also a passionate woman. Studies show that the vast majority of problems in the home have been linked to finances and sex. In most cases money is never a real issue. With today's generous credit plans, low monthly rates and high yields on savings, a family with almost any level of income can tackle the American dream. What usually happens to the perfect Christian family is: the man works, the woman raises the kids. On Sunday she takes them to church while the father vegetates in front of the television or plays a round of golf with his business associates. Now, as my aerobics teacher says, golf is no sport. They might be handsome Christian gentlemen basking in the American sunshine, wearing spotless pastels, but these same men couldn't for the life of them lift their wives over their heads. I'm not suggesting bring on the barbarians. I'm simply saying both sexes need to be strong, not for war, but if that's the only way we can think, fine, because the real combat is love and that's how I want to die...in the midst of carnality.

141

Most ladies who've had children avoid two-piece bathing suits, for good reason: to prevent the sun from falling out of the sky. The flubber factor, a natural disgust. What I'm trying to say now is that physical fitness is an important part of the sensual side of spiritual life. Christian women must be stunning to compete with today's sexually suggestive, amoral beer commercials. If we don't the family will fall apart. We're never going to be nineteen years old again. There's got to be something that turns their heads back to us. It's not cosmetics; it's sexual ability, passion and fury; it's professionalism and style in bed. As many men will testify, the old gals know what they're doing and are far better than the young squeamish ones. We'll go the whole mile, and then some. We purr with sincerity. We all know why that is. A lady's vocabulary eventually gets reduced to the same humbling word: we're horny.

WHAT SOME PEOPLE consider politeness, others consider criminal. A man speaks for a woman. Crime. This happens every second of the day. She'll start with a green salad, the man says, and she'll conclude with a cherries jubilee; in the middle of those two dishes my soft, mute companion will have the salmon, to look at, not to eat. Later he says, I want you to have my children. She thinks, Sir, is that an order? He thinks, At ease, Private.

Now the reverse. A woman speaks for a man. What's wrong with this vegetable? All stump. Is the man ill? Nurse him. Is he stupid? Is he a donkey? Pull off his face. Make the dummy explain. Men open doors for women, pay the motel bill, Kick General Generous in the butt. They do it all because they're frightened. They can hide it all they want but we see it in their eyes. They're dilated and watery. My husband's unable to come to the phone. He's under the weather. He thinks the world is trying to rub him out. His throat is clogged with soggy bread.

I'VE ALWAYS BEEN taught that the imagi- 143 nation is dangerous, that it could burn you up. I liken it to a big scary hole, a pit. You could fall and bang your head. Why would you want to get lost in that? This is why I stay close to real things. If it bothers a writer to be asked: What's your writing based on? Where does it come from? I say, writers of the world, borrow my hanky and shed a tear, because it's a legitimate question. I think about those types of questions but never ask them directly. I'm a curious person. I wonder about many things, and yet I keep them to myself because I consider this woman in here (I'm pointing to my heart) respectful of others. My curiosity is based on caring, on love. A Christian woman must never grow weary of that word. If I know a story is real I can offer more sympathy to the characters. Isn't that what a writer wants, a little pity? They fill up legal pads and tap away on keyboards in their solitary confinement, and their only reward is that readers praise them for being an effortless and articulate version of what God had in mind. A mindreader. Characters inhabit books. They walk around in my head like unwrapped mummies, dazed and embarrassed, with no flashlight, stripped of their words. I cry about real blood. I fall apart when something solid disappears. My sister's feet turned black and eventually fell off from toxic shock. That's bad. I say all this because I am one of the regular people of the world, a person who appreciates culture, who lives and breathes, works, does what she's supposed to do each day before settling into bed with a few prayers. But now I'm suddenly one of them, a writer, one of those people I wonder about. This is a story.

I've always found the print of my typewriter exciting; it's so commanding, each letter and word standing there like an army of bugs in a straight line; write half a sentence and I'm that much closer to heaven. I knew this would happen. I talk all the time but it doesn't mean as much as seeing it on the page. There's something unsettling about the writing process, such a grim and confusing experience, but when it's over you have a crisp ironed shirt. The world salutes the dazzling surface. I mess up when I talk. Just little unconscious mistakes. I hear myself say *uh uh*, *you know*, *umm*, and *so* a lot. It doesn't sound clean. I could probably cure myself of this by just slowing down. That's how I stopped myself by stuttering. People used to look at me like something was coming out of my nose. All that did was make it harder for me to get the words out.

AT THIS POINT I find it necessary to write in the third person. The crucifix Loretta wears on a chain around her neck was a gift from her mother and father on her sixteenth birthday. Bless their hearts. And like any piece of jewelry worn around the neck of a big-breasted girl it falls right between her breasts. It tickles but never pokes. I don't wear this cross around my neck as an ironic statement, like many young women today, she says.

145

Loretta is thirty-seven years old. The same age as me. She is a fun person. That's how she describes herself. I'm fun, she says. I'm different than most people; I enjoy life, not like my brother who cherishes death. His heros are murderers. Does Loretta look old? Yes, her job and her rigid haircut, which one crude man described as looking like a hydrofoil, also give the illusion of her being middle-aged. Loretta will live to be a hundred. Check out her butt in the shower after tai kwan do class. She can tighten that jiggling mass into two adorable fists and flatten any threatening pig with a flying butt slam. She takes pride in fighting off the depressing destruction mother nature has unleashed on her body. Every morning she does fifty squats and hip thrusts, leg lifts, crunches and propeller twirls. She applies ointments and ice packs. But it's her crucifix that protects her from the assorted evils of the world.

LORETTA'S LIST OF EVILS. She prepared it last night during an ordinary moment of self-doubt. Lists always calm me down.

1. Stabbed to death in my sleep, heaven forbid, by a deranged person, or by some hired fellow: everyone has an enemy.

2. Run down by a drunken motorist: these things are commonplace in Los Angeles. There are so many ways to be killed, so many anxious maniacs looking for the opportunity. It's unpleasant to think about but no one can say that I'm a naive woman.

3. AIDS, brain tumor, etc.

4. Crushed or swallowed in an earthquake. I'd include volcano eruption, tornado and monsoon, but this is the wrong part of the world.

5. Electrocution (with so much electricity floating through our world, and all that moisture, I'm surprised more people aren't zapped; I won't allow my husband to blowdry his hair while I'm soaking in the bathtub).

6. An airplane crashes into our house. Crazy thing to have happen but it happens to someone every year.

7. Taken for the wrong person and drugged to death with heroin, or just killed with poisonous vapor, after I continually say I don't know what you're talking about—like what almost happened to the actor Gene Hackman in the *French Connection* movie.

NO MATTER HOW many companions appear to be by her side Loretta walks the world alone. But isn't it the same for all the good and bad people of this world? We're alone, thinking our own shaky thoughts. And aren't we all bad in that special way, under the wattage of supreme truth? That's why Jesus is here in the first place—to remind us that there is always something we've neglected, someone we've deceived, hurt, even crushed; to keep us on course; and most of all, to dim the hardship of loneliness. Every step is a treacherous undertaking, a solo plunge, and often we go down. But (and here the *but* is so large and extreme your modest and grateful narrator is starting to quake), for the faithful the opposite is the case. When you have Jesus in your heart it's like you're in the midst of an invisible army. And as long as you remain pure His orders are clear. The commands are sublime. Turn around. About face. Forward bliss. The devoted are under a constant state of supervision—at once being led as well as followed. He knows how easy it is to wander in the wrong direction. When you land hard on the pavement the

Lord's Holy Shovel scoops you right up. The divine muscleman. How many miracles are you willing to accept in the wink of an eye? Why not an infinity? *Infinity:* another word of everlasting meaning. It is the biggest word, with application directly to the Almighty. Infinity is only understood by those who are willing to open up and fly with Jesus. The Light He emits is a radiant beam so bright, pure, and immaculately round like a spot for center stage. I tend to think theatrically, having spent a good part of my life singing and dancing. Often I find myself lost in the glory.

Loretta says: My husband's name is Bill but I call him Wolf; he's so hairy, and he growls. When Wolf asks me to kiss it, kiss his organ, suck his cock, I mentally ask Jesus a question. Is this okay? Do you mind? And I always get the same answer. First nothing, not a sound or sign, the silence of consideration, as if He was uncertain. Even though Jesus is perfect that doesn't rule out time to contemplate. Then, before too long I hear His unmistakable whisper. He says, Drop an octave, sweet Loretta. Get down on your knees and suck Wolf. And so I do. Wolf, wolf. It makes sense that He would specify knees. The standard position of His disciples. I respect His hesitation in answering, His weighing of the issues. I believe only the greatest men admit their worldly quandries. My husband is not such a man. He's sweet but his doubts are hidden in the vault. But he's not like most men, who're quick to force their opinions down your throat. In time Jesus will strike the roughneck down. That pleases me. Christian justice. Know-it-alls getting their comeuppance. I always envision lightning bolts zooming down from the sky, plunging into their heads and shoulders and going straight through to the toes, like a shish kebab. Skewered alive for piggishness. But Wolf's not like that. He's not a bastard asshole. He's trying; he's learning to listen and I love him for it. Wolf is old-fashioned. That's difficult for him to overcome. He's still getting used to the new ways of male tenderness.

So I take Wolf's cock in my hand and I feel the world change. Suddenly I know what it might be like to be Jesus. For Him it was healing people and walking on water. For me, what was once soft and mushroomy grows fat and stiff, and because of my saliva, glows like a movie theater hot dog. A miraculous event. I feel safe and happy with Wolf in my mouth. I look at him and he shuts his eyes. When I bite, his closed eyes tighten. His chapped, puckered lips fan out and quiver. During the magnificence of such passivity he trusts me not to hurt him. He opens his eyes. He sneaks a glance, blushes, turns away.

Loretta says: My husband breathes harder. The tops of his feet bead up with sweat. That's how I

149

know he's enjoying himself. And his face goes pale. He asks me to take it all, and again I wonder, is this something Jesus would sanction? I wait for an answer. I hear a firm yes. I close my eyes and press on until my nose bumps into pubic hair. With all of my husband's sex in my mouth I think about Jesus impaled on the cross, the back of my throat struggling as my heart carries me through. It can't be helped. That's what it's all about. Jesus was, and is, a medium of love. The pain He suffered, how poorly He was treated, how little He asked of others and how much He always gave (and continues to give). The job only gets harder. I love you Jesus. Wolf squeezes my breasts. He likes it when I make choking sounds. He says that's erotic. And Wolf in turn grunts and howls, which gets me even hotter.

With His good looks I wonder about all the sex Jesus must have refused. Those paintings of Him naked, floating about in heaven with dutiful angels, or on the cross, and the focal always being the abdominal region, and then of course the eye continues to fall. They paint Him with a tiny cock so no one will contemplate giving Him head. But it doesn't work. Over the years we've reconciled size; it's no longer an issue. What are the citizens of the world supposed to do with His image? We will always think of Him, and His Cock. We can't help ourselves.

Wolf is like Jesus. They both have beards. Wolf can sing. He sings while he does the dishes.

Jesus was also a singer and played guitar. That seems obvious. As Wolf pushes his cock to the back of my throat with his cute flabby hips, both hands holding onto my ears, as if my head were a steering wheel, my mouth the ocean and his cock the modern oar, I come up for air. I think to myself, Cum in me, Jesus, cum in my mouth. Give me life. Scorch me with your pearly lava. I promise I'll swallow this time.

Squash

OUR BIRTHDAY BOY is burning his T-shirt and sneakers and hair with my best box of wooden matches. He pretends he hasn't done anything. I see the damage, I smell the sulphur. He's not going to get away with it, not my boy, birthday or no birthday. A boy should be thankful for being allowed to live another year; this one's nine, a devil in pre-pubescent clothing. No one should disrespect the gifts of earth. I snack on several doughnuts and a bowl of chili and discover six pennies missing from my dresser. This is all in one day; the clock hasn't struck noon yet. Something's got to be done, something firm and unforgettable. Punishments are unavoidably wicked. So I call the criminal forth and he denies all charges. But I am the judge. I tap knuckles on my gam and whisper, Guilty, justice must prevail, and sentence the pyro-thief to a paddling. I grab my trusty broken broomhandle, and the naughty boy runs around the apartment screaming; but he can't escape, the back door is dead-bolted. I waddle as fast as I can, whacking him a few times to tame him. I get him into position in the family room. Each swat only makes him wilder. What's a two-hundred-pound mother to do? Here's what I do: I toss the stick down and flip the creature on his back and sit on his chest. I shove an unsavory sock into his mouth to cut the volume, pick up a *TV Guide*, see what's on tonight and this week. I become engrossed in a witty article about some new trends, and then a very important exposé about the hypocrisy of beauty pageants. Then my other little offspring comes fluttering in and demands I get off her brother. I say, who do you think you are? Do you want to be next? She says, Mom, you're hurting him, he's not breathing, he's blue, he's not alive. And she pushes me. She defies her mother. Then she picks up the phone and starts dialing, looking at the emergency numbers I conscientiously taped to the phone. I say, Put that receiver down right this second. She whispers, Please help me, my mother is killing my brother; our address is 250 Heliotrope; I'm his sister, please come quick. She doesn't hang up. Very nice performance, little lady. No allowance for you. You are grounded. She presses the receiver to her chest and starts sobbing. I've gotten so comfortable I can't rise off our birthday boy to slap the nonsense out of the brat.

153

On My Birthday

THE FIRST THING I think when I wake up in the morning is how much I love school. I tingle all over at the thought of walking the mile, which seems more like ten, through my nice neighborhood of noisy, stinky dogs—especially in late spring when it's three million degrees out and the asphalt exhales in my face. Or when it's hailing, sometime after the new year, and the stones gingerly tap my skull. I love that. Yes, girls and boys of the heart, I feel a closeness to my environment, and this meditative feeling enriches my fond personal association with Ralph barf Waldo Emerson, the transcendental humanoid we're currently force-fed in American lit.

I can see why Nathaniel Hawthorne, who I really think is the coolest guy in the universe, thought Waldo was a good poet but a bad philosopher. Nat thought Waldo's brain was too out there (my words). Every so often he'd poke his noggin out to touch something real. But Waldo never touched anything, especially not me. No, sir. All I know is Waldo's book of essays gives me a headache; it's medicine for martians. He's gross. I'm with Nat, who's totally hip. Nat's the only guy from the nineteenth century who I think was cute. No long, scary beard just a brilliant and dreamy face. When he got older he grew a mustache. I don't mind. That's what a cute guy can do. Make his face look weird and he only looks cuter. His story, "The Birthmark," is the coolest; and "Rappaccini's Daughter," purity and poison, my favorite themes. God, and *The Scarlet Letter...* Puritans bug me. The next time I see a snail creeping out of a bush I'll make sure I step on it, and call it Waldo.

155

People don't like sarcastic girls; boys especially don't. They get freaked out. I don't know why. People act like you're a blob of writhing plasma if you don't talk nicey-nice. Be a lady. Oh, okay, I think I know what that is. We have this thing between our legs; it's spelled with the letter V or the letter C (only nasty people use the letter C to say it) and it's a receptacle of something even worse. I think I know what that is, too.

A cock.

First period is Danbom's Dirt Farm. That's horticulture. I took it because I heard you could grow marijuana. Not true. I also took it because I heard you could hide out in the greenhouse pretending to water something and no one would bother you. True. My cabbages are dying. I'm not too upset about it— they're smelly and give me gas—but Danbom is. He cries all about all our dead vegetation. He says we must care about plant life in order for the world to continue. That makes sense. Little does he know that he's got thirty teenage vegetables lounging at attention in his classroom. Danbom is a sweet man. He's kind of nineteenth century but I could never fall in love with him. Danbom's tranquil, works hard, carries my bags of peat moss and steer manure, helps me dig and I'm pretty sure he won't fail me. Danbom thinks I'm a good girl, even if he's afraid to look at me.

My bedroom, which is where I am at this precise second, is painted buttercup. I can picture a bunch of paint experts sitting in a room and one of them urinates in the corner and the president says, Brilliant, Dave, very mellow, very now, that's the color we've been searching for. My parents didn't exactly consult me on this hue. It's the same color as the snoozing drool that leaks out of my dad's open mouth each morning. Everything in this house is buttercup. The curtains, the carpet, my mom's nails, her clothes, her car. Everything.

ANYWAY, I STARE at the ceiling in my bedroom longer than I do at any other single surface in the world. That must say something about my life.

Like maybe I have the emotional fixings to be a nun, a glorious and memorable nun. Headmistress, of Our Mother of Good Counsel. Yes, and they'll call me Sister, Sister Jill; and I'll be tall, practically six feet, my head as high as the top of the lockers, and when I walk down the hall my black shoes will click and echo as I go, and all the young girls will think, I hope Jill holds my hand today and kisses me. Compulsively, the girls tell me all their troubles and everything they do with their boyfriends. We giggle together; they ask me for advice. I encourage them to do naughty things, to experiment. No, I don't see Sister Jill working out. She'd get thrown in prison and then she'd hang herself.

157

I'll admit that I'm a little bored—not to be confused with serene, which I'm not at all—and curious: I'm willing to take a chance. Hey, how else will I grow into a worldly woman? I've got to do strange things: eat food I might not like at first but grow to appreciate; travel this country, then Europe—those are the obvious things. A worldly woman has a *broad* mind and if she ever makes a stupid pun like that she coughs slightly, covering her mouth of course, and moves on.

Actually, I'm just spacy and explosive—that's mainly what I am. And today I'm sixteen years old. My birthday. Thank you, thank you, no autographs. Old enough to drive a car with a permit, if I had one, and I will next semester. I'm employed at the Good

Earth as a waitress; a job that teaches me about the world in the worst way. It's made me a misanthrope. I want to strangle the groveling slobs who snap their fingers and wave their coffee cups. That's why I stare so much now. To calm down, also to fall asleep, wake up, pray, flirt, figure and brood. And most importantly, to forget about eating. I'm skinny enough but I always feel fat.

I see the ceiling in my bedroom as a giant astrological map, with all the cracks and paint peels serving as the secret forecast of my future. And today it tells me, very plainly, to explore my brother. Go, denotes the new little crack that blossomed over night, go. It wig-wags the message like a commanding finger.

Interesting. And so I will obey.

A bathroom separates my room from Dennis's. The rooms are exactly the same size, each with a window looking out at a giant grapefruit tree that brushes against the glass every night and recommends that we never drop our guard. Wise old tree. The only difference in our rooms—we both have tons of posters of rock bands—is the lack of special markings on his ceiling. From what I can tell he doesn't have a single scratch up there, just blank, smooth space, and it's my belief that my brother's life will move along the way—smoothly, without doubts and fears. Nothing disturbs him. He reads the paper in the morning: murder, flash flood, tornado. He digests it all with a cup of coffee, without a gasp of profanity, the only language I truly appreciate. I'm not trying to say he's a callous slime. He's wonderful, I love him. He's a sweety pie.

I've got to get up.

The way I see it I really don't need to wear any clothes. I can be naked because it's my birthday. But it's chilly, so I'll put on my uniform. Black bra, aqua panties, black jeans, black Stereolab T-shirt, purple socks, black Doc Martens. My one-woman funeral procession.

Down the stairs, tear up the town.

Dennis is in the kitchen, slumped over a plate of scrambled eggs. He's finished reading the news-paper; now he's plowing through *Melody Maker*. I tousel his hair, strangle him and kiss him on the neck; release him, back up, freeze and say a little more formally than usual, Good morning, Dennis. He doesn't look up.

He doesn't say anything.

Are you going to school today? I ask.

Time goes by, then more time. Nothing. It's not that I'm speaking too softly; this is just the way he is: ultra removed, pretending not to hear, like his hearing is shut off, and it kind of is. He only responds to music. That and boy talk. He likes to talk about gigs and girls with the guys in his band. Wicked guitar solos, a hot new monster drummer, a totally cruel bass player, a girl singer with a lips big enough to

159

climb on. I'm used to Dennis not speaking to me. A lot of men do that. It's an ancient method of torture: the silent, you-are-invisible treatment...until you die. I'm not a masochist, but honestly, it really doesn't bother me. I know he's listening and I'm pretty sure he loves me.

Dennis, it's my birthday.

I've been excited about it for six months and now that it's here I don't know what to do.

I say, I'm a simple girl. You know that. Do you know what I'd like to do today, right now? Dennis turns a page of the magazine. Walk around the block. We used to do that a lot—race each other—remember? You'd always win. But let's just walk. What do you say?

I know this sounds pretty dumb. It does to me, and it must sound a lot worse to Dennis, but if you think about it, doesn't a walk also sound freaky and fun? I think so and I'm the birthday girl, so what I say goes.

I guess not.

How about a big kiss on the cheek or maybe on the lips? A brotherly kiss on the mouth? Would you do that for me? Please. That's all I want. It won't cost you anything and it'll only take a second or two. I'm not expecting any fancy girly gifts, I swear; I just want something from the heart, to know that you love me and think I'm the coolest sister in the universe.

I know Dennis loves me, but I have to say it out loud to believe it, and when I say it I can feel my brow and upper lip creeping toward each other in suspicion. I'm prone to days when all I think about is how lonely and ugly and loathsome I am, no matter how much evidence there is to the contrary. Dennis and I haven't been in a big fight in weeks. We're getting very good at respecting each other. Dennis looks like a statue of flesh. Should I grab a mirror and jam it under his nose to see if he's breathing? He continues to read. I'm a girl bugging him, the creepy sister. His face is like a pink sponge, drawing in all the latest music gossip. He lives off that stuff. What local bands have been signed. Are the Breeders breaking up for good this time? Is Kim Deal off heroin? I read it, too. It means a lot to us. Dennis is eighteen. He's tall, skinny and pale. He's got a long, turned-up nose that looks like a ski jump. His hair is black (mine's dark brown), his eyes are green (mine, hazel). Dennis plays guitar. His band is called Buttafuoco. Dennis feels small in the big world but I think he's a giant in a tiny one. To me Dennis is like Peter O'Toole in *Lawrence of Arabia*.

Our parents left for work an hour ago. In their absence I've decided not to send me to school. Even though friends might sing to me and someone might have bought me a cupcake, I'm not interested. Today I study at home.

How about a backrub? You owe me at least ten. That would be an acceptable birthday present. I'll take off all my clothes, and then you massage me. I'll run upstairs right now and get out the baby oil.

He turns a page of *Melody Maker* and stabs at the lump of egg he amazingly continues to eat. A yellow morsel separates from the mass. He brings it up to his cheek and holds it there. He reads on. I light a cigarette and throw the match in the sink.

What if we go into the den and snuggle together with all our clothes on? I promise I won't tickle you.

I blow a few bad smoke rings but I got the French inhale down pat. He's not looking anyway. He bites the egg, swallows it and lowers the fork.

Dennis, listen to me. I'm serious; stick your hands in me. (Now I'm mad.) He holds a piece of burnt bread next to his face.

Drop the toast and crawl over here. Put your hands to good use. Do you understand what I'm saying? Let's see those gifted fingers of yours. I want you to squeeze me till I pop. Pluck me good and hard. Strum me like you do your Stratocaster. Hit a few extreme chords—blow out my amps.

I run the tap water for a second, to drown my cigarette. He bites the toast, bites it a second time, and a third, until it's gone, and then he picks up the fork. Now I'm twirling my favorite curl by my neck. Dennis coughs.

I want you to make me moan, because I'm going to make you stutter and cry. Come on, brother boy; I'm hot for you. I can feel it down here.

He coughs again.

I rub my crotch. It feels good, surprisingly, since I'm standing in the spazzy kitchen I'm currently growing up in, and my morning incest speech, which I'm smack-dab in the middle of, is causing me doubts. I've touched myself plenty of times; it's a wonderful treat, a shock that it works, but now I see the three-fold problem: my brother, myself and what to do. All the elements are so detached from each other. I hear myself talking and I think, What, What is it? Are you serious, Jill? Do you really want to fuck Dennis? And I think, Yes, yes I do. I am serious, and a little scared. I'm on a mission.

Dennis reaches for the glass of milk. This he holds like a chess move, with his eyes fixed, of course, on the magazine.

Since we've grown up, Dennis and I rarely see each other naked. Once he looked up my dress, or I stepped over him while he was fixing something on the floor, on his back; he grabbed my ankle and wouldn't let me pass, then he looked straight up and said, Wow, Jill, and then he sang, You're not a kid anymore. I've seen him in the bathroom, his flat chewable butt, and his cock pressed against the basin as he shaved. It's nice. The little elephant trunk.

Start real slow, you know, first lick me all over, my legs and arm pits, flick your tongue like a nasty little lightning rod on my C, then tear me to shreds.

For a moment Dennis glances up at me, like he's about to say something; he lets go of the milk, which he still hasn't taken a sip of, sniffles and wipes his nose; then looks back down, flips several pages at once and brings the same hand back to the glass.

I want my head to come off, Dennis. We're going to exchange heads. I'm going to suck on you with your own head, pry off the tip of your cock and wring out all the cum. Every drip drop in my birthday gullet. Between my teeth, I'm going to shoot the cum back into your eyes. Remember, we switched, so the jet stream will be accurate and forceful because it'll be your boyish ability spitting into my astonished eyes. Lucky me, I catch the cum twice. Of course I'll be rendered temporarily blind. Help, help, I'll say, and you'll have to save me. Wouldn't you? Don't boys like to save girls?

Dennis turns a page of the magazine, gulps half the glass of milk and groans slightly. He's probably thinking, Jill, go to school and be with your friends. He licks off the milk mustache.

Dennis, frisk me. Fuck me standing up. Get me against the sink here. Come on, scare me. I want to see the pictures of us as boy and girl scouts fall off their nails...the lightbulbs to burst...I want all the plaster in the house to drizzle inside the walls.

Zero.

Dennis and I are real close. We kiss each other all the time. When I slip my tongue inside his mouth he balks a little. He's kind of shy. I've been doing it for a couple years and he's never socked me for it. He's braided my hair a couple of times. He does it tight.

Dennis, you're going to be real wacky with your cock inside me. How much do you want to bet that you'll think you're flying? We'll be doing hyperspace. I'm going to steer you into a mountain. When you squirt inside me I'm going to scream the dead awake and lock up your happy cock. All the grapefruits will crash through your window and roll under your bed. I'm going to bronco-torque your cock to a zillion RPMs, until you spaz out, and then I'm going to flip you over and lick out your ass. And then...

Would you please be quiet? Dennis says without looking up.

I will pause but I will not be quiet, I say.

Isn't this a male fantasy, women begging for it, saying wild things? I have to step out of myself for a second. The aggressive woman laying her cards on the table. All I want, all she wants, is sex. She's an animal. The classic tiger image. Isn't that why men are aroused by leopardskin fabrics? So what keeps my birthday experiment from working? It's not that Dennis and I are siblings. That's a separate problem. If Dennis said similar sexual things to me which I might consider erotic, that would be a female fantasy, wouldn't it? I'm not sure. It would probably be horrible, no matter how much I was attracted to the guy. It

165

would be like a parody of love, or a denigration of what's magical about touching someone. The available words aren't satisfactory. Coming from a man, those kinds of sentiments only sound like pig talk. There's a vulnerability in sex—*don't nod off on me*—that exists even in the most comfortable, trusted exchanges. It's a spell that's easily broken. I'm hardly an expert but I've picked up a few things from feeling so strange and sad about it, and occasionally great. I don't see anything inside this situation of mine that makes it particularly tricky and, so, bound to fail.

I open the fridge and pass my eyes over the milk, the eggs, orange juice, yogurt, apples. There's broccoli and carrots in the crisper. No Pepsi in sight. The same disappointing garbage. My mom shops for people who don't live here.

Dennis, look at me for a second.

He doesn't.

I lift off my top and unhook my bra; I drop them near my feet.

Dennis, I want you to come over here and kiss my puppies. I hold my tits. I squish them up a little. I say, I'm worried about them; they're very friendly but they're so sad, so lonely. Won't you give them a little kiss? Puppies die without affection. Come on, pet the puppies. Look how droopy they are. They're crying.

Inside, I think he's laughing, and the surface has changed slightly. There's a tiny smile on his face I don't think was there before. I pick up my bra and throw it at his head. It lands on the magazine. He says, Cut it out, and brushes it to the floor. I take my shoes off and place them in the sink. I do the same with the rest: socks, pants. I'll leave the panties on. It's more romantic when a guy takes them off.

Let's go into the garage. I want you to fuck me on the worktable. Your cock is a long fat puppet with a silly face and it's going to whisper globby poems to me.

I snap my jaw a few times, like a cartoon carnivore. I'm going to tear off pieces of your flesh. You smell like corn bread. I'm hungry for starch.

He closes the magazine and stares at me. He folds his arms. Now I got him.

Work the land, Dennis; we're going to fight like the labor union, put in the hours—it's the only way to salvation. Tug on this hair, yank it all out. I hold my head. And here, I say, rake this. I hold my crotch. Come on, Dennis, get up, nail me shut with your hammer. This is the only way I can legitimately miss Danbom's class. We've got to plant a seed at home.

Dennis stands up. He takes off his shirt and throws it at me.

I'm a little witch. I groan. I'm going to die now. I'm ready to die. Someone kill me. I'm dying. You're killing me. I'm killing you, you ruthless bulldozer, you Rachmaninoff, you fucker, you fucking bear. I love you so much, you evil priest. I love your stomach and legs and saggy sack. Reduce me to nothing with your big green eyes.

I charge at him like a wild boar. Dennis catches me. He holds me. I feel dizzy and crazed and then suddenly sick, like I'm falling, and, God damn it, I start to cry.

Time Bomb

I GO TO THESE meetings a couple times a week for people who drink too much. Wanda's Wagon. That's where I met our great blonde leader, Wanda. We sit in a circle and talk it out, let it fly. Everyone calls me the Time Bomb. I break chairs. A vehicle for venting anger, she says. The group encourages me. I laugh. Disguising pain, she says, not the healthy smile I want to see. The chairs don't actually break—they're metal—but they make a lot of noise. The joyful sound of mayhem.

Wanda is very beautiful. She's not perfect in the *Playboy* sense of the word. She doesn't curve like the great ones and her rear end doesn't raise off the ground like the tail end of a hot rod, but she wears excellent clothes: a red dress, a black dress, tight

slacks, culottes. Her legs are strong like a thorough-
bred's. She has wavy, animal hair. When she looks at
me I feel electrocuted but I go on living. I speak
frankly: Wanda discomforts my erogenous zones.
She's so tough she makes me swollen without even
laying a finger on me. She's got hidden erotic powers.
She says the only important thing is to get healthy, to
take better care of myself, to stay on the wagon. Well,
I got news for her: I love that wagon; I want to climb
right on and ride it all night.

Wanda gives the special losers, us people who
pretend we're going to *off* our precious little selves,
her home phone number in case of emergencies. So,
being as disturbed, lonely, confused as I am, I call her
several times each day, especially after the bars close.
I have to speak with the human vitamin, my emotional coach. The 110 percent I'm putting out to the
world has dropped below 50. She starts up with, I'm
bothering her, that I'm abusing the privilege, she'll
see me tomorrow, sleep is good. This ticks me off.
Sleep is fucked. She told me I was handsome. It
would bother any man. My phone calls are soon
answered by her husband, who insists I stop calling or
else he'll be forced to call the police (ooh, guess I'll
go to bed now), but instead all they turn me over to is
the recorded message about not being in—which is a
lie—and to leave me name, the day and time I called.
This brings out the fang in me, so I repeat my name,
the day and time, and the year, make and color of my

balls, until the tape runs out. I know she's listening. Listen, I need her. Does anyone know what that means? And I think she loves me. Her eyes pop out at me like they were meant only for my two eyes. She's just shy.

This is her way of saying come and get it, ravage me, Foghorn. So I do, late one night. Using the intuition that got me this far, I know her husband is out of town. I don't even break the door down. She lets me in, backs up, looks at me like, Baby, it's you, and then she tells me to go, to get out of here, she's tired, early appointments. She looks scared, sexy. I tell her busy people are pompous—everybody's busy; I'm busy now, I'm swamped, but we'll straighten that out horizontally. When I grab her face and kiss it, the head spins away. Very responsive. She runs across the room like we're supposed to play tag and I'm It, but instead she opens a drawer and pulls out a gun, a .22. She points the little dinker at me, shaking. Déjà vu: I haven't had a weapon pointed in my direction since the war. Continuing to operate on instinct I advance with caution. I got my hands in the air, smiling my adorable smile. She keeps saying, Stay where you are, leave, and I'm warning you. At this point I can't keep from laughing, it's too funny, cop-talk coming from Wanda. I take possession of the firearm. She practically gave it to me. The mating ritual can be so complicated. I tell her I want to be inside her now. I heard that in a porn film and it drove the actress crazy.

Wanda runs for the door. I shoot her in the back. Oops. I had to stop her. Makes sense. She turns around and calls me a prick. I shoot her twice more, I'll tell you where: in the left tit and in the crotch. That's where blood appeared and started to spread. I didn't aim exactly. I just squeezed. I wanted the gun to keep her from leaving, to stop her from calling me names. That would get any guy mad.

The woman behaves like someone taught her how to die. Why does that surprise me? Everything she does is rigid and predetermined. Stagger, stagger, plop on the ground, inaudible mumbles, groan. I ask her where her car keys are, but of course she no longer speaks English, even though she can still blink. She crawls out the door and down the driveway, stops on top of a pile of leaves when I trot by. I try not to look at the twenty-foot smear of blood. I drive off in her yellow Pacer. At home—at the bar—it's not even close to 11 P.M. The guys don't believe me. They say, No way, Pal. You don't have the walk of the killer—as if it should be something special—nor the eyes.

Celery

THINGS ENTER MY HEAD whether I permit them to or not. My mother is always the first to barge in through the cranium. She seeps in without knocking, sits down and tells me to clean up my cortex and olfactory bulbs. I was born on December 9. I must've been baking since March. My father was dogging mom in springtime. There I was, a science project, camped in my mother like an Eskimo warding off a storm in an igloo. A long summer and fall. Sugar Ray Robinson was the middle-weight champion. Nowhere to go, nothing to do, just kick and do headstands. She warm, that mother tummy. She had my sister fifteen months earlier. The civil rights movement was underway. Passive resistance was constantly met with white violence. Twenty years earlier the country was elated by Jesse Owens humiliating Hitler. Welcome to the world. My mom told me she didn't want another varmint so soon, but there I was. I continue to have the same experience today. Not yet, could you wait a few more minutes please. *No*, I always think, can't wait another second, eat my shitter pudding now; but it's *yes* I notice my mouth discharging. I raise a celery stalk to my mouth and chew it up. It is a succulent, hardy, biennial plant of the family *Umbelliferae*. I put the encyclopedia back in its place like a good boy. I don't let my toys sit around. Looking up things I don't know (everything) helps me grow. Uh huh. A tiny piece of celery is stuck between my teeth (between the lower central and lateral incisor, to be exact—the teeth I use for biting and cutting, for identifying objects in my mouth and for nibbling). They complement the immobile set of teeth above them. I return *SORD to TEXAS* to the bookcase. Teeth work like a mortar and pestle. Thirty-two teeth for adults, twenty for children. Fifty states in the union, fifty stars on the flag. The United States fought to separate themselves from England but all we did was imitate them. That's American life. Copy what you kill. Fuck like a dreamboat. Hump like a madman. A woman, the opposite of a man, was in a chair, on her butt, wearing a blue bra, Ms. Ocean. I was standing there like Mr. Erection. She said, Yeah, fuck me. The words, of course, frightened me. I held her legs wide apart, bending my knees, pumping down like some sort of whacked-out oil rig dance. What were we doing? Fucking can seem so stupid, but in a great goofy way. I did feel like I was searching for oil. The oil of her soul. Yes sir. We were scrunching up our faces in righteous mutual freak out. She stuck her index finger in my mouth and said, rip it up. I sucked her finger for a few seconds and then pulled back, and yelled, Oh, God. Afterwards I was jamming grapes into my mouth and choking on them but also trying to talk. I pictured someone banging me on the back, but what I preferred was the Heimlich maneuver. Heimlich's first and middle names were Henry James. He might still be alive, but for the purposes of objective reporting let's assume he's dead. The next word in the dictionary, after Heimlich, is a great one: heinous—and would you believe it, its derivation is German. The celery remained stuck between the aforementioned teeth for several days. In a subtle way it changed the way I look. I never looked in the mirror to see exactly how; I just knew. I looked more sullen than usual, my cheeks sunk in. It did something strange to my upper lip and altered the shape of my chin. I pressed the tip of my tongue (the apex of my important accessory organ) against the trapped celery fragment. I moved the tiny vegetable, which was fast becoming a comfort, up and down. It helped me think. I continued to star in my sex life. I ate more celery hoping that by introducing new stalks the lodged fragment would be released. Then one day, possibly on the fifth day, my tongue (it had purpose, beyond its usual duties of giving head and tasting food), obsessed with its pale green play thing, my tongue, getting stronger by the hour, suddenly, without warning, removed the piece of celery, leaving my mouth 1000 percent empty. My tongue went back to its favorite spot and there was no little flicker to tease it, just the smooth backside of my lateral incisor. My tongue returned to its old inert self. Another man would've flossed but I chose the road less traveled and experienced pleasures of far greater magnitude.

Accessory

THAT DAY, EXACTLY one year ago, the Fourth of death-trip July, I should have walked forever or never gotten off the bus, waited till it circled the globe and returned to my old neighborhood in Santa Rosa. It was the day my parents had had it up to their eyeballs with me (which my mom frequently illustrated by drawing, with the side of her hand, like a salute, a line at the bridge of her nose). I'd look at the measurement and then at the top of her head and think, I have four inches to go. I was eighteen, a miraculous number I'd waited all my life to reach, legal for everything except booze, which only made me gag. I repeatedly violated my parents' rules, so their commitment to me terminated (dad's word). They wouldn't tolerate another second. They felt taken advantage of, like I was forcing them to harbor a felon. Yet all I did was partake of the herb that's been with us since the dinosaur. A misdemeanor.

All my spare hours were spent in the chicken coop, where I'd smoke pot. The hens sat in their little boxes and laid eggs—they looked higher than all the stoners in school put together, with their tiny red eyes fixed on nothing—while the chicks and roosters skittered about in protest of my invasion. I'd sit on the floor, surrounded by the true smell of chicken shit and think about nothing. I was reading about it in school: existentialism and Zen. Perfect subjects for a zombie like me. I'd think about the future, and the future seemed scary but cool. It would just happen, no matter what. That was radical.

My pot was stashed in the pocket of an old coat underneath my desk, loose joints in a metal Band-Aid container and the ultimate hash-oil doob in a hollow pen casing that lay inconspicuously beside a pile of seemingly ordinary pencils. My mom found everything and threw it out. She said she didn't want to see that stuff again. I was going through tons of Lifesavers and Visine. A couple days later I came home from summer school freshly toasted. My dad forced me to take a speed-reading class. He said a competent man should be able to read a book in ninety minutes. I'm in the kitchen, hunting for scarfables, reeking of pot. My mom smelled the trail. She said *out*.

My mother's finger pointing at the door was followed with an attack by stiff, tranquil fatherman, who was purple with rage and armed with the shovel. Mom ratted. He was there like surrealism. An absurd and morbid flash. Men dressed like him only touch shovels in photographs related to real estate ceremonies. He blasted me in the knees, the left ear and the balls. When your parents throw in the towel, or in my case, cream you with the deep scoop, it's curtains. Wild time. I tried to talk them out of it, blood leaking out of me, but they wouldn't listen. They'd turn me in but I could go free if I left them now. Start walking.

I took a Greyhound. Very scenic. Bill, a sort of friend from school, met me at the bus station. It's smack dab in the middle of Hollywood.

Bill is a strange guy. The first time I met him I watched this football guy beat him to a pulp. Bill taunted the guy, saying football players were not as tough as they acted. He said they were all faggots. The last word hovered in the air. Very odd thing to say for a million reasons.

Bill's comment aroused the football player. He licked his lips and methodically unbuttoned his jacket. He pulled the neck of his jacket through a rung in the fence and rubbed his hands together. He approached Bill as if he were a meal. Then he punched him at least ten quick times in the face. Bill just stood there, didn't move until it ended.

179

I watched from the other side of the fence. It was ugly and weird. It was also strangely great. Then Bill turned to me. I thought, Oh, fuck, what does he want me to do? He was a cheerful bleeding mess. He was dazed but seemed proud of himself, that he survived, or that he could take more, or that it actually felt good. His lips were blasted open. I tried not to laugh. He was pleased I was the audience.

I accompanied him to the nurse's office. If he had died or something and I walked away I could've gotten in trouble. He knew my name, which surprised me and it made me feel great, but I didn't want to talk. The football monster would whomp on me if he thought we were friends. I just thought I could help by being a presence, hopefully an invisible one. His nose wasn't broken. The violence connected us in a tiny way.

Hollywood's intense. There were drug dealers and drunks, odd mothers, children and garbage all around the bus station. It was neat. We walked around to Bill's place. He lived around the corner.

Bill lived with Bobo, this massive black-bearded creature. He's probably seven feet tall. He's part tree, part ape, which are two of the many reasons he is boss. I needed a place to crash. Bobo said I would sleep on the couch. I rolled my stiff neck that I wrecked on the bus and acted grateful. One false move and who knows where I'd be. I picked at my scabby ear.

The next day Bobo told me I could stay as long as I liked and that the cellar was mine if I was for real. What a freaky question. Maybe I wasn't so real. Bobo's the kind of guy who can tell. Being and nothingness, I guess.

Bobo told me I'd need money while I was here. I pulled out my wallet and counted. I wasn't sure how many days eighty-five dollars would last. Bobo snatched it out of my hand and said not very long. What are you going to do now, he said. I told him I didn't know. I felt puny. He said he was a talent agent, did I have any talents?

That's how I got started in show business. Like they say, it's all who you know. He said the best way to start is through modeling. At first I thought I'd never do naked stuff. I don't hate my penis, I'm just not the kind of guy who falls in love with his own thing and names it Python or Chuckie.

Bobo said, Let's see your cock. I thought I didn't hear him but I knew what he said. For a change I wasn't going to say *what* and piss someone off. I unlaced a shoe and he said Fuck the strip tease, just the cock. I obeyed, moved fast. He looked at it. He said, shake it a little. Good. Lift it up. He nodded, then said, Nice balls. Now turn around. Great, hairless, you'll pass for fifteen. Pimples too, excellent.

Okay, jump ahead. Now I get modeling jobs all the time and as of last week, two feature films, *Rearview Mirror* and *Frosted Flakes*. My stage name is

Steve South. I wanted something cooler but Bobo said, Uh uh, go plain. Photographs of me, my torso or just my cock, next to a male or female model's wide open crotch. The photographer takes a bunch of pictures real fast. At first I felt like I was at the doctor. There was alcohol and cotton everywhere to keep surfaces clean. The other models and I hardly touch each other. I hold my own cock. They open their mouths like baby birds wishing for worms. Sometimes I'm supposed to cum, sometimes I'm not and I wish I could. The other models get a bonus if I cum on their faces. A hundred bucks. They call that the money shot. That's what sells the magazine. One photographer shot my cum in sequence, with a special device called a motor drive. He shot ten pictures with super high-speed film. In the magazine the pictures were laid out on a grid—my cum traveling from box to box, like a UFO crashing toward earth.

I've been in eight magazines so far. Five ads and three layouts with little stories about being lost or sidetracked on my way home from school, or being the winner of a spelling bee. I have copies of all the magazines. I had to buy them. Bobo gets them free but he won't share. I don't even recognize my own cock. Change the angle you normally look at yourself from and suddenly you're a stranger.

I try to empty out my mind like a Zen master, until this wild movie starts in my head. I see things I hope come true, like me being famous, surrounded by other famous people, everyone being nice to me, calling me their friend. (That's what's most important. Being nice and being friendly.) The phone rings all day. Surprisingly, half the calls are for me. I'm pretty nonchalant about it. The other half are for Jack Nicholson, my new best friend. He thinks I'm a real kook. Jack worries that he's a *has been*. I reassure him that he's the ultimate *is here* dude. He's grateful. We laugh.

EVENTUALLY another movie. A detective pushes me down into a chair and asks me what I know. Start talking, he'll say. He'll circle me, hands in his pockets. Do yourself a favor. You're not a bad kid. Let's hear it.

183

I wish that would play out right this second, rather than me sitting in the van, as always, in the middle of the desert, holding the steering wheel, waiting for Bobo and Bill to finish.

I'm sure the detective says you're not a bad kid to all the guys my age. If I was a girl he'd call me young lady. If I were chubby he'd say, Listen, fat boy, we'll starve it out of you. But I *am* a bad kid and he knows it. So he starts out by lying and expects me to do the same: lie for a while and begin to tell the truth in a few hours. His job is to get the story out of me, a confession. Say I did things or saw the guys do things.

I can see the empty room, no windows, a light bulb in my face. Cliché interrogation. It starts out nice with ordinary questions, but when I don't cooperate he'll come down hard. If I yawn and look away the detective adjusts my head by clamping a huge paw across my face, turning it back in place.

I want to talk, I'm just out of commission. I'm losing power. I'm a space cadet, I say to the detective. And he says, That's cute. I keep thinking he'll be fatherly (please, no mustache).

No matter what the detective looks like, he begins to seem attractive and those looks pull everything out of me. But when I slow down and forget things he gets grumpy and bullish the way fathers do when a son doesn't follow orders. Dads always make you feel like you're in their secret marines.

My father is so American it's scary. At a baseball game during the national anthem he knocked my hat off my head and said with his jaw locked up, Show some respect. His conversations rarely ran over three words. I wonder if most men identify with eagles, see themselves as strong independent birds that swoop down to pinch and kill anything weaker than they are.

The detective says, Listen, cockroach, you're in so much trouble you'll be lucky if you get twenty-five years. I'll slam that nose of yours against the floor so many times you'll never breathe through it again. No one knows what you looked like when you walked in here. On the other hand, if you cooperate... things could lighten up.

The detective's name will probably be something like bonebreak. Don Bonebreak. A name you couldn't believe and couldn't forget but that's actually real, that would get me giggling and into further trouble. I'll have to force myself not to look at his nametag. Bonebreak, Ballwalk, Fuckears, I'm dead.

MOST OF THE TIME I feel like an emotional cripple. I sit in a chair frozen for hours, without a thought, feeling or impulse. Except maybe being nervous. Months without a single hit of pot. I'm way too nervous. I don't have the shakes, I don't—I'd like to believe (I know it's not true) that I'm a calm person— it's just that when I pour my first cup of coffee I'm usually thinking of the night before, what my friends have done, or what to eat. Eating improves things.

I'm always hungry for heavy, sweet things: Belgian waffles, apple fritters, French toast, pecan pancakes. My hand tips a gulp of coffee my mouth isn't ready for—and spill, down the front of my shirt. I walk through the doorways and slam a shoulder on the jamb, or I step backward and bump into a table and knock over a gin bottle or an ashtray.

People don't trust a man with a spotty shirt, even if it's sporty. Dirt is what people notice and they immediately think you're a low-class, insane criminal. My mother believes messy things are constructs of the devil. Bleach is Lord. People see dirt and ask themselves what you've done. They transform into instant inquisitors: What unusual behavior caused those brown marks, green streaks, red spots? Isn't it obvious? Gravy, a roll in the grass, a mishap with a knife. But I haven't done anything wrong. I swear. It's only coffee.

When the terrible things happen I stop thinking. I go away to a place in my brain that's quiet and full of light or something, a place where plants grow real green; damp crisp air all around my head. The only red I see is the red of roses, or blushing faces, or candy apples. No blood—I stay away from that. I force myself to believe that I'm seated beside a big honest tree, not inside Bobo's van. I breathe and make sure to blow the air out with a little noise, so I know it's been done.

I don't think about what's right and wrong too much. I couldn't. Still, what happens around me seems a little unfair. It's ugly no matter how you look at it. If you have a chemical imbalance you might disagree. You'd say what they're doing makes perfect sense, that the ends justify the means. Violent people always like Nietzsche. That's what I say is off about my friends. Internal malfunctions and the wrong books. They're haywire but they muster fierce convictions. They get fiery.

My family doesn't have a history of insanity but there's something about all of us that's slightly off. It makes me think someone burned the mental health records. Once my older brother Fred and I were standing on the roof, checking out the situation. We just started climbing and found ourselves up there. We weren't talking about anything. The world was shimmering and loopy. We were tripping on windowpane. Just standing there, on the roof, feeling hail-the-conquering-hero mighty, and then all of a sudden he grabs me and throws me off. I land in the grass on my face. I look up at him, not sure what was broken, thinking he'll start laughing like it was a joke but he just stares at me. Then he says, You won. I'm like, What? What did I win? He's like, You won, period.

Bobo, Bill and I drink a lot of coffee. I'm responsible for making it. I brew it weak. That's the way they like it, so it looks like tea. I prefer it extra strong, so it's fudgy. Pulls me temporarily out of foggy brain sludge. If the coffee's too strong Bobo heaves it against the wall.

I clean up everyone's spills because I dislike messes and I'm sort of the maid and don't pay a regular kind of rent. Disorder worries me, makes me feel frantic and lost. No big thing. I don't know where I picked up the cleaning habit. It's easy to say, from home, from one of my sisters, from mom, but I think it's something new. I was a slob when I lived at home; I worshiped the confusion of the chicken coop. Now I clean so I can float through the room easier. If I didn't think of these discreet forms of protection, like cleaning, I'd sink to the bottom. I'd drown.

I wash everyone's clothes. Bobo and Bill mostly wear dark colors. Black heavy-metal T-shirts of bands they've never heard of, to make them look like roadies, black jeans or these permanent-press work pants called Dickies. After a night out they're stained, soaked and stinky from head to toe with thick red blotches; sometimes there's a mysterious piece of goo caked to a pant leg or an even bigger chunk nestled in a cuff. Real spooky. A piece of flesh or something from the inside that bursted out. I switched from Tide to advanced-formula All. It just seems to get everything cleaner, smelling nicer. When I overcrowd the machine or dump in too much detergent—two bad habits I can't seem to quit—the granules never dissolve. They form little chalky pockets of detergent that stick to the fabric and I have to send it through another cycle. If they wore white clothes I'd be handing everything back rust and pink, the dye job of the century.

Zen master Suzuki said a beginner's mind is very important, so I keep telling myself I don't know anything, I'm a beginner, a baby, and you can't expect much of me. I will do things in a fresh way. Pour a glass of water. Cherish its existence and clarity. Breathe, sip the water. That's all I need. Hello, water, I'll say that right to the glass.

No one ever listens to me. That's okay. I don't pray for that to change, since I hardly ever say anything. Don't speak to be heard. I'm here to learn. A man's accomplishments are not measured by how big a mountain he climbs. It is the beauty of one step, the grace of smelling and seeing or something.

One day in the middle of the afternoon my father, I mean Bobo, screamed for me to get the hell over here. I didn't know what I did wrong. He kept yelling, Hurry up, I want to show you something. When I walked into the room he was standing at the other end naked, cranked on gin. One hand was on his hip, the other cupping his balls and cock as if they were going to drip on the floor. He said, Get over here, man; check this out. He pulled back his foreskin. Look at this, he said. I saw the image of a fly tattooed on the head of his cock. Great, huh, he said. Hurt like a motherfucker but it's a work of art.

189

DON'T JERK ME AROUND, you little shit. Bonebreak won't go for my speech. I don't want to hear your cute Thus Spoke Cinderella story. I'm your only conscience. You're an animal who lives with other animals. You get me? Tell me who you really are and what really happened with those people. I know when you're lying.

OK, no movie. Sunday night is usually the night they like to go out and harm. They say they're doing God's business on the closing of his big day but

Bobo and Bill never attend church. Their religion is killing. They take a hustler, the unnatural fish (their words), and smash him up. They say ancient Rome fell because of fags. Buttfucking screwed it all up. But they like to buttfuck too, so I don't get it and I don't ask. I've seen Bobo fuck Bill. Bill suck Bobo. Bobo and Bill fuck a retarded boy they call Cornhole who smears shit on his cock. I've seen them tons of times. It's pretty boring, even when they do things with bananas or spaghetti or bean dip or mud—it's like they were in kindergarten. Bill will say, I want squishy fuck. Bobo wears diapers and smokes a cigar. He takes Bill from behind and shouts, Squeal bitch. Bill baas like a lamb. He can't even get that right.

Bobo says we kill them because of the look on their faces, their goddamn smiles, their insipid artificial happiness or their pathetic depressions (this is him, not me, he says); we cut away the lips because they're always pursing and mugging (you should see how peculiar lips look separated, in the dirt, with no chin or upturned utopian nose to pucker with) the cool pseudo-rebel poses, pretending to have a corner of the world to themselves, their lame wiggle-walk, the use of the pinky finger to stress a femmy point, the sweet drinks, the maraschino cherries, the whole cueball baldness thing, leather jackets, backward baseball caps, rock 'n' roll T-shirts, how they look at my girth (Bobo's fat) and insinuate that I should lose weight, fucking dead ass. But the real reason we kill is the joyous sound of a human's squeal. I grew up in Arkansas, and when I hear suuuuuueeeeeey, all I think of is pig farms, which translates into gutting and fucking, feeling the kill in your hands, the begging, the squirming, the twitching, grooving on a palsied, wonky death. It's like part of me.

I'M THE DRIVER of this little family of men. The driver, not the mascot. It started one day when Bobo asked me to drive him to a burrito stand. He told me to pull over by the bridge, leave the car running. We were directly over the freeway. All I could think of was getting thrown over the ledge, and being run over. I didn't want that to happen. I'd rather not die at all. I'm familiar with being uncomfortable. I don't mind it. Bobo told me to roll up my window. It was one of the hottest days of summer, close to a hundred degrees. Cars zoomed below us. Maybe another driver will see what Bobo does to me, if he does anything; but I guess a witness can't bring you back to life.

As usual, I did what Bobo said. I rolled up the window. He's older than me, smarter and he must've known what he was doing. He talked about the human body, it's beauty, his fondness for gymnastics, wrestling, archery, his dead wife (so he was married once). (First you go, Huh? Then you go, No, marriage or divorce doesn't unpsycho a psycho.) He talked about the Bible—he's writing a new one and if I had typing

191

skills he'd pay me to transcribe his notes, but I'd have to promise not to read any of it, just type. He related everything to pipes, washers, nozzles and flushing action. He said I meant a lot to him and never to leave, that we're friends and he needed me, to break our rapport would be sinful, grounds for aggravated tumult.

I said I needed him too, I don't know why. It just came out. I was trying to be friendly. When someone says something nice to me, I say something nice back, even if it's a lie. I remember I was wearing my usual T-shirt/sweatshirt combo: the inner layer red, the outer, yellow. Friendly colors. Even in the summer I wear a lot of clothes—making believe I have a thicker skin cheers me up—but on that day I felt the heat moving up my legs and down from my head, meeting in my chest for a thorough baking. I was going to change form. There was no air. I was damp all over. Sweat dripped from my face and poured down my armpits. My thighs were weak and soaked. Bobo turned on the heater; he continued to talk about cleaning up society. He said compression coupling was useless without the shutoff valve of the almighty loin dredger. I began to shake. He kept telling me not to look away, eye contact was energy, pupil-to-pupil brainslaw, don't deceive with the averted gaze or else I'll be forced to reroute your falsehood. Tears and sweat fell into my eyes. Things got blurry. His eyes were oval smears. I looked at the bridge of

192

his nose, focused on a glacier-mole inside the crease. Then there was another big silence. He stared at me like a laser. I faint a lot: when I'm scared, when I feel claustrophobic or when I'm real high. I had about two seconds remaining on the clock. My arms and legs tingled with fright volts, terror was shooting out from my fingers. He was going to pop me into his mouth like a Twinkie. He was talking fast: police, righteous burning balls, intelligent men produce less urine, seagulls love corn chips, tomato juice stings cock, wack-off to giraffe killing. He asked me why, if the temperature was so high, I insisted on wearing my sweatshirt? I didn't know. No reason. So I took it off. I wasn't insisting on anything. He asked me why I wore a shirt underneath that. Bobo gets angry when I don't answer smartly, when I say, I don't know, or yes, in a half-assed manner. I opened the door and fell into the street. I sort of fainted but not completely. My eyes were open but I couldn't really see. The asphalt and chance for air brought me around. Bobo walked to my side of the van. He probably thought I was faking. His boots are black with layers of grease and other gore stuck to the toe and laces. I assumed they'd kick me in the face. I deserved it for being so uncertain and queasy. If he liked me when the lesson was over it would be worth it. But he helped me up. He said he knew he frightened me. He wouldn't let me go. He grabbed my shoulder with a monster hand, a thumb and forefinger gouging my collarbone. If I tried to wrestle out of his hold it would only get tighter. Just as the pain sent me to the pavement again he stopped. He said that fear was as stupid as a sneeze or a burp; that he'd teach me how to obliterate it. I said thank you. He tousled my hair. I could breathe without worrying. We jumped back into the van and took off for burritos.

His van is fixed up real posh. Black velvet floor to ceiling, for those who ride shotgun. The back is lined with industrial rubber so any mess can be hosed down. The van seems huge from the outside but inside it's kinda cramped, unless you're lying down and then it extends in every direction like a tree house. There's a teardrop window on one side and the words KEEP ON HACKIN' stenciled on the other side. It lures the metal boys.

I drive so Bobo can get a good look at the boys on the street. It's strange because in one sense hustlers are Bobo's favorite things in the world. He chews on them every single day, stinky-boy wack-off yum-yum, but then he changes and it's like he's ashamed of himself. He plays with them and acts babyish, does gorilla nice-nice, then look out, he bonks them over the head and drags them to the slaughterhouse.

Every Sunday here's what happens: At 10 P.M. we drive around and look at all the boys on the street. Bill in the back seat, Bobo in front with me tapping drumsticks on the dash. Bobo selects the kid. His favorite age is sixteen—hair black (straight not curly), no body hair, talkative, muscly, big cock, of course. Once the boy steps into the van his life is over. Bitchin' van, they always, always say to me, like it's mine. I used to say thanks but now I don't. They instantly trust Bobo because Megadeath is stretched across his stomach. Are you HIV neg? Bobo asks. Sure the hell am, man—neg I mean, they say and then jump in. If one said pos he'd live longer. I keep driving. Bill yells *bingo* and knocks him face down into the back and throws on the cuffs and then starts giggling like a slobbering goon craving din-din, and starts taking Polaroids. I'm like trying to act expressionless or normal, just look straight ahead, but all the car talk is insane. Bill says, We're going to fuck you and then we're going to cut you up with this (shows cleaver) or maybe blast your ass with this (shows gun). If it were up to me I'd kill and then fuck you—decisions, decisions—save the funnest stuff for last or just dive into blood world. I pretend I'm wearing a walkman and I've got it cranked up to ten. I take the 5 north into Palmdale, same exact route every time. Bobo pulls out his notebook and squeezes into the back. He starts reciting: And the Lord harkened unto Bobo, afix your anger with rubber washers so the truth will not leaketh forth. (He wacks the notebook on the kid's head for emphasis.) Behold compression coupling and its wanton fury—and

195

thither were the flock of bitchy little runts gathered—he pokes an edge into the kid's eye (screams). I get off at Avenue L and make a right on Clacker Gulch, turn off onto the dirt road and take it to the base of the hill—always deserted. The recitation continues: ...and they rolled the stone from the well in the field, and lo, another fuckable shit. Surely thou art ready for the bone of bones. Ye shalt replenish via rejoice of liver removal—sacrifice the tyke. I park. They drag the boy screaming from the van. I turn on the radio. Bill's got him by the throat with a chain leash and choker. Bobo carries the lantern and dufflebag full of instruments.

According to the wallet his name was Thomas Humphrey. They go behind the big rock. It usually takes two or three songs.

I just sit. I never touch anyone. If I did I know I'd feel bad. Detective Bonebreak, if you say Bobo and Bill are animals, that reminds me of what Suzuki says: the shepherd must never try and control the herd; they will only be unhappy and rebel. Instead, give them a larger field to mosey in and they will graze as they should. And that's what happens. Bobo and Bill, on the other side of the big rock, chewing on their cud.

Movie: My plans were to rent a corner of my sister's property in Oregon for zero dollars and build myself a fine little abode one day. The entire dwelling would be one giant greenhouse. One room, no material objects—just a mat for me to sleep on and plants everywhere, wiggling in harmony, soft leaves touching my ears every time I turn my head.

No movie: They return giggling and breathing hard, drenched in blood. I turn the radio off during the Beastie Boys' "Suck My Kiss." Blood's splattered across both their faces. They smell like a sulphur-cheese concoction. They describe it to me, how the body hissed after the first big puncture, all that pressure built up from panic. Bill cut off two fingers and put them in the boy's nose. He pulls the rest out of his pocket, Want one? He said his blood tasted like Snap-e-Tom. Bill shoves in a cassette, *Who's Next* by The Who, and starts singing along to "Boris the Spider."

We're all starving. Burritos. I don't even have to ask or be told. I head straight for Poquito Mas, my favorite stand. They wait in the van, I place the order. Same thing every time. Three asada burritos, three carnitas tacos, and one tamale for Bobo. I walk to the liquor store and buy a case of beer and two bags of chips, one nacho, one original flavor.

Bobo is silent, almost comatose. Normally he's full of commands—turn left, slow down, pull over, stop. Bill asks Bobo if he'd like a chip. He turns away from us, stares out the window. We finish eating and continue to drive. Bill expresses himself:

I want to electrocute somebody. I want to see someone shake with a thousand volts. You know, we never really torture anyone anymore. Am I whining? It's too fast now. Boom, they're dead. Maybe it just used to seem longer. Torture takes patience and planning for it to really turn out great. We need water, or a stun gun, shit to wake them up, keep them alive before wipe out. We're too much into immediate gratification. Also we've turned into outdoorsy types. Desert rats. Remember the shit we used to do in the basement?

Back to me. It's July, a Wednesday or Thursday, I'm not sure. Bank of America says it's 12:46 A.M. 78°. There's lightning in the sky—not the strobe kind but gigantic lightning bolts. One single drop of rain hits the windshield, no more. I decide against wipers. Bill continues:

On the other hand, nothing more pleasurable than a no-nonsense decapitation. A clean slice of the blade. Ooh, look at this charming club steak. He'd look sweet on the rotisserie. Pull over.

I obey. Bobo leans back in his seat. Bill lunges forward, plops down on Bobo's lap and pokes his head out of the window like a giraffe.

Hi, you know how to get to Magic Mountain from here?

Yeah, the boy says, it's kind of a long drive. Are you guys lost? He's wearing baggy Levi's and a black T-shirt pulled behind his head so his stomach is exposed—washboard, black hair, pimply, maybe seventeen, or maybe twenty-five, really hard to tell.

Yeah, we don't know where we are. Where are we? Bill rolls his head back and forth in mock derangement.

The boy's mouth opens a fraction. Almost smiles, looks confused. He laughs for a second, then says, So.

Want to go for a ride? Bill asks in his baby voice. My daddy here... (he kisses Bobo on the forehead; Bobo doesn't react)... will pay for all of us and let us drink beer.

Sounds pretty cool. Should I get in back?
Definitely. He climbs in.

199

PLEASE BE A COP. I can't take this. Be Bonebreak. Shoot them.

I want to go to bed.

The Future

INSPIRATION BASHED ME hard in the thinking cap this evening. I was at the movies watching Errol Flynn do his thing when suddenly a thought came to me. My dead wife—she's dead but she doesn't have to be. Not anymore. I can bring her back. Not with hocus pocus but with hog's blood.

I poke a bunch of holes in her arteries and drain her of all that embalming fluid, and then I inject her full of hog's blood. I'm certain it'll work. Then I connect her veins to mine, and in this way she will return.

Here are my goals. I'm going to start a construction business as well as a taxi service that carries people to every part of America at the lowest price imaginable. These automobiles will hold more people than eight trains combined, and move twice as fast as a rocket. I'm going to build three additional stories to my present home, for recreation. I envision a movie theater, a tennis court, a bowling alley and swimming pool. I'm going to leave additional space available for whatever my wife needs.

I am the smartest man on earth. I was dead for an entire week with a gunshot wound to my heart. The only way I can be stopped now is by a mighty blow to my skull with a hammer.

My son will assist me in this enterprise but at the moment he can't think of anything except all the singing planets in the sky.

The Present

MY SON THINKS JUST because his mother is dead that we should bury her, before we've tried everything. She is dead, that much is true; but what isn't a hundred percent is whether all other avenues have been fully explored. The world is a slippery place; dirty and confusing. Death might seem like some kind of one-way street but who says you can't float back when the traffic is light.

In one sense I understand my son trying to get his mother into the earth before she rots. But disgrace is not always avoidable, especially when it comes to the preservation of life. The boy's got the right idea: put dead people in the earth, and through that procedure, hold that spiritual creature dear and tight, or they us. The relationship develops unexpectedly through absence; a constant buzz ensues; the ground you walk on is a perpetual reminder. In your sleep new situations are played out. Everyone knows how a ghost, or a gang of them, can stand on your bed and disrupt your sleep. They flush the toilet, try on your clothes, pinch your groin. Once a ghost gets used to her new found form she develops peculiarly normal qualities. She whines a lot and gets strangely insecure. She begs for attention and after she's gotten it, of course, she pretends you don't exist.

What we don't put down into the earth we burn up. People worship ashes, or at least savor the small gloomy urn. I'm aware of the laws and customs of our society. The problem is, we as people can't lay down our own dead. A citizen is not allowed to bury his own, personally and privately. The most painful moment in my life has to be made public and cost me more money than seems right. People who live in this area make arrangements with the incorporated father-and-sons team in town. An Irish family. Callahan. A pack of drinkers and roughnecks. They bury everyone. A monopoly on the dead. In one sense my son is saving me a lot of money. $1568.90 to be exact. I don't like the idea of anyone other than myself stripping my wife naked, sponging her clean, dressing her in something pretty and pulling a smile back on her face. We can dig our own hole and ease her in ourselves, but if we're caught I'll go to jail. They might even think I killed her, since a real doctor has yet to examine her. Hospitals treat patients like worthless furniture. I'm a Christian Scientist.

Matter is the unreal and temporal; it's mortal error. My wife died all by herself, in a chair. Spirit is immortal truth. That's what she needs right now, my concentration. Calling on a doctor isn't something we do. Love always has and always will meet our needs. Here's how I feel: someone's measuring spoonfuls of salt into my poked-out eyeball.

I ONCE KILLED a man for digging a hole. A stranger. I was drunk. I saw him digging. It got me angry. I can't explain it. The hole was wrong, stupid looking, and it was a very hot day. Why should anybody be digging? While I was in jail I thought of all the times I've wanted to kill someone—at least once every day. I'm always blowing my stack. Temper's an odd little toy. At that crucial moment, right before you do anything, and then once you've decided to go ahead and do it, killing is an honest reaction. You're pissed and the other guy needs to be quiet. But I tell myself, No, don't kill every day; don't kill everyone who upsets you; don't throw pitch forks at the faces of strangers who look at you with insinuating eyebrows. When I was my son's age I thought all the time about killing my parents. Amazingly enough I didn't, and they didn't push me down the garbage disposal either. They could've; I was their little one. All I did was eat. My indigestion alone turned their lifestyle into a sour drama. So now I say to myself, You are a fortunate man. Think of how terrible it would be if I were a day-to-day killer, a drug addict of blood? It would bore me. It would be like weighing diamonds full-time, or being a professional smoocher of bikini models, or a vagina doctor to the stars. Imagine getting used to that? Excuse me, Ms. Gina Lola Osayno, could you spread your awesome hairlessness a bit wider, I'm having trouble reaching your inner sanctum. And then she says, Doctor, is my cunt still pretty? An unnamed leading man is coming over tonight to put out my smoldering inner heat. She looks at me like that man might be me and I say, unable to hold back a yawn and bored by the same trivial questions, Yes, I say, yes Tina—I mean Gina—your vulva is arresting. But killing once, and learning from it, will turn a man around. And it's wisdom that sets the tone.

205

ALL I KEEP THINKING about is the expression, Thou shall not inter until attempts have been made to restore life through all the subtle, vague and often abstract means of osmosis. It echoes through my head like the lyrics to a song I like, that I think is speaking to me personally, but after a hundred efforts of listening still don't fully understand. Osmosis: not as complicated as one might suspect. A mixture of the physical and the spiritual. People die of cancer from standing beside smokers; others are poisoned through a handshake. The same can be said in reverse. A dead person can be rejuvenated if placed properly beside a vibrant, utterly living, human being—and that thriving entity is Yours Truly, speaking now.

THE MOMENT MY WIFE died my son took an interest in geology. He turned to digging. Right now he's in the yard digging harmless little holes. He knows that a deep, narrow rectangle will set me off. The shape of a grave; the squaring off of the human body; not much different than a large bathtub; it's impossible to overcome.

The deeper a man drives his shovel the more he sees how the earth looks, how it changes. We need to know that, men do. I sit here with my son in mind and I speak for our species, the male subdivision. Here is a rock: dry, coarse, with tiny granules covering the surface. I flip the rock over and it's caked with dark wet earth, the first layer. There are worms crawling about, performing an unknown task. Let's not go into that. Jab a shovel down and you come up with more damp earth. Somehow the earth is moist all by itself. Inner rivers. The soil of the earth is worth comparing to the soul in a man's body. The earth is comprehensible even if the book my son's reading makes no sense to me, whereas the soul inside us is a total mystery. I see the earth as a big body, an old one, something everyone calls Mother. She grows things all the time and yet remains round; to keep us honest she throws a lightning bolt and a hurricane our way, then an earthquake. Still round, a floating ball. My body burps up all kinds of surprises, which I observe in the same way—with curiosity and fear.

My son smears earth on the wall opposite the fireplace. He uses his fingers and a sock he no longer intends to wear. At first I was disappointed with the picture. I expected something beautiful or realistic, like a house, a tree with people beside it, a dog. All he made were layers. He used water to thin it down. When I got angry at the picture he told me what it was and I got embarrassed. Stupid me. He was drawing the levels of the earth itself. All the joints and cracks, the interesting ripples and strange crumbling things. I look at this brown mess, which could be seen as an offense to decent living conditions, and I think, the world is basically brown: whiskey, beans, steak, hash, my clothes, hair, eyes—and when I am regular, an encouraging number two.

I point at random to a paragraph on an open page of my son's textbook on the kitchen table: the new minerals that develop during chemical metamorphism are, as a result of directed pressure, dominantly flat, tabular or elongated bladelike forms. The common minerals that have these shapes are muscovite, biotite, chlorite, talc (a hydrous magnesium silicate) and a bladed variety of hornblende. The technical world is an excruciating place. You want to know more and all you're left with is a hostile vocabulary beating you on the head.

I JUST BATHED my dead wife in epsom salts to get the final impurities out. The burping drain reminded me of her own booming burps and

207

made me think that she was already back with us. I let
her drip dry in the tub for ten minutes before towel-
ing her off. I carry her into the room, gently drop her
on one side of the bed (clean blue sheets, like the sky)
and leap over her onto the other side. I strip. I lay
down next to her. I feel like we're two glazed, spiral
logs cooling on the rack. This procedure isn't totally
out of character. When she was alive I used to make
love to her when she was sound asleep. I told her that
one afternoon and she said, Fine, just don't try and
stick you-know-what in my mouth.

I roll my wife on top of me. Her eyes are
closed. She's gained weight. I wrap my arms around
her, kiss her; no tongue, a simple peck. I tuck her face
into my neck and breathe the life inside me back into
Meredith. You're such a wonderful woman. Wake up,
Sweetheart, I say. Make me look silly. I push her off
me and roll on top, kiss her again. Come on back, I
say. Here I am, wishing you were here, no place like
home.

208

Dear Dead Person

MOST PEOPLE'S LIVES are drab and uneventful. They enjoy the excitement of an accident. It gives them something to talk about and makes them feel important because they were there. Then of course, there's morbid curiosity. It is one of the less attractive qualities of human nature, but we all have it in varying degrees.
                    —*Ann Landers*

Dear Dead Person:

I just wanted to write you a little note to say how happy you made my family and me. We were on our way home from a short vacation to the lake: the kids, in the back seat, sunburned from head to toe, complained about this and that—how much longer till we get home; they were starving as usual (so was I in fact); and my wife, Sam, was losing her temper—a slap to someone's face from one of her two quick hands was imminent. All of a sudden the traffic brought us to a stop. Your accident was up ahead. At first we didn't know what it was. I thought, it's probably no big deal, just a small wreck, a dinky fenderbender. About a mile ahead I noticed a distinct swirl of blackish smoke poofing into the air. A good sign, I thought. Twenty minutes later, everyone's patience tested to the max, our car crept up to the scene. What a joy it was, and well worth the wait. A person rarely gets to see such a sight.

My kids were adorable. They continued to yell and scream, but very intelligently, I thought. My son, Eric, requested I turn down the radio. I recall I had it on an Oldies station. I turned the damn thing off.

Dad, Eric said (the boy is seven), wouldn't it be neat to make cars that were smashed up like that one to begin with? Then when the car crashed it wouldn't look damaged. Or maybe someone could design cars that looked upside down.

I think the boy could market that I idea, I do. I said, that someone is you, Eric.

My daughter, Nina, admired the way the firemen walked—big methodical steps. Sam asked me if the sheets they put over the dead were made specially for that purpose. I didn't know, so I just said yes.

The family came alive as I've never seen before. Sam yodeled in fits of happiness. She reached for my hand and squeezed it. Then she slid over, grabbed the back of my neck and kissed me roughly on the mouth. Wow. Then she gave me an infinitely powerful look with her big browns. I love that woman.

I often wonder what it is that kids enjoy today, and I haven't the faintest idea. What with the video games, the strange movies in sequel, their private undecipherable slang, who can keep up? Here was something we could all appreciate. A current event—or a tragedy, if you will...depending on how you see it, of course.

I count six bodies, Daddy, Eric noted.

Look at that naked man, Nina said. He's bright red, with little black specks.

211

I slowed down. That was you. I stopped the car. You must've been alive at the time, even though that seemed impossible. Your left leg flinched. Today's paper reported that you died as soon as you arrived at the hospital. Your torn-up legs were bent in such an abnormal pose. You looked like one of Nina's dolls after Eric has inducted it into his army. I'm really sorry. I assumed every bone in your body was broken. One fluid action causing all that damage. I expected the car behind me to honk. But I looked in the rearview and they were just as engrossed as we were.

Eric crawled half way out the back window before Sam reeled him in. Please, Mommy, he said, I want to touch the dead people.

Listen, Eric, I said, we are here and that's the important thing. Appreciate this moment from where you are, be grateful you can see this much, and anyway, son, the police won't allow you to touch the dead—you have to be a member of the family to get that privilege.

But that's not fair, he said.

Okay, that's enough, I said.

Clearly it was time for us to move on. And so we did. I just want to say, for myself, that the best part of the experience, if I may be so bold, was your face. It wasn't a face. Just raw, living meat. Do you know what astonishes me? Take away one layer of our skin and suddenly we look like monsters.

Respectfully yours,

MAN OF IMPORTANCE

Of the stories collected here, the following have been previously published: "Pushed," *Amokkoma* (Cologne, 1993) and *Santa Monica Review* (Fall 1990); "Truants," *Santa Monica Review* (Fall 1992); "The Present," *VLS* (Fall 1992); "On My Birthday," *BOMB* (1991); "Real Me," *Loaded* exhibition catalogue, Richard Kuhlenschmidt Gallery (1989) and *B City* (Spring 1988); "Artist and Fly," *L.A.: Hot and Cool* exhibition catalogue MIT List Visual Arts Center (1987); "House Monument," *Forehead* (1987); "Dear Dead Person," *L.A. Weekly* (Dec. 4, 1987); "The Future," Issue (1987); "Time Bomb," *Tongue* (1986); "Ardmore," *TV Generations* exhibition catalogue, Los Angeles Contemporary Exhibitions (Feb. 1986); "Museum Boy," *Journal: A Contemporary Art Magazine* (Summer 1986); "Expressionism," *Journal: A Contemporary Art Magazine* (Spring 1985); "How I Made Certain of My Art," *High Performance* (1983), *Postille* (Berlin, Summer 1993), and, cut up, as answers in a mock interview with artist Thaddeous Strode.

Various parts and versions of "Dear Dead Person," "Flesh Is for Hacking," "Squash," and "The Why-I-Love-Violence Speech" have appeared in *Brooklyn Review* (1992), *The Crunge* (1993), *Farm* (1990), *Frame-Work* (1990), *L.A. Weekly* (1986), *Cindy Bernard: Ask the Dust* exhibition catalogue (Richard Kuhlenschmidt gallery (1990), *Spazio Umano* (Milan, 1986) and *Helter Skelter: L.A. Art in the 1990s* exhibition catalogue, The Museum of Contemporary Art (Los Angeles, 1990).

To order HIGH RISK Books / Serpent's Tail:
(US) 212-274-8981   (UK) 071-354-1949